I0667060

TO BOSTON
With Love

To Boston With Love
Copyright 2019 by Murray Segal

Printed in the United States
by Piscataqua Press
32 Daniel Street
Portsmouth, NH 03801

ISBN: 978-1-950381-19-7

TO BOSTON
With Love

A Patrick Ingel Investigation

MURRAY SEGAL

To Janice Wayne

Once again in my hour of need you are there, to edit and to keep the Toshiba going. And to find the book after I have carelessly pushed the wrong button. Talented, and a good writer in your own right, you have come through again!

All My Love,

Murray

CHAPTER I

Gineen and I left Norwich, Connecticut the very next day after we were married there. I am a private investigator named Patrick Ingel. We were married in the rooftop suite of Roger Jones, our boss at the Casino Royale in nearby Voluntown. We left quickly, packing a few clothes and personal items. We said goodbye to Roger Jones, my former client at the Casino Royale in Voluntown, Connecticut. Roger had grown to like us both, to the extent that I saw tears in his steely eyes when I told him that Gineen had breast cancer. My job at the Casino had been to catch a gang of thieves who had been robbing the Casino. I was successful and had been rewarded with a million-dollar fee – the most money I had ever dreamed about and never expected to earn in a lifetime.

Now we are heading to the Dana Faber Brigham and Women's Cancer Hospital in Boston. Jones volunteered to find us some housing units within walking distance of the center. In addition, he made a reservation for us at the Inn at Longwood Center where we will stay on arrival. As you might guess Jones had more money than he could spend in a lifetime. Not so obvious was the fact that he had more or less adopted Gineen and I as the children he never had.

A million dollars sounds like a lot of money, but it shrinks to about a half million after taxes and that would not buy us much of a house in the Boston market. Besides, that would further diminish our stash. I need to find work quickly to survive, leaving Gineen by herself for long periods of time at the beginning of her treatment. This is something I vowed I would not do. So, I accepted Roger's kind offer of a place to live. If I live to be two-hundred, I know that I will never find a man as generous as he is. Furthermore, he fixed us up with a financial advisor; help I had never needed in the past, having had no assets to speak of. As we start to pull away from her condo in Norwich, I look over at Gineen and see her sobbing quietly.

"Are you in pain?" I ask.

"No. At least not physical pain," she says, "but this has been my home for several years. I feel like I am leaving my entire past behind me."

"It's the future that I am focusing on," I explain while putting on my signal. "We are in for a tough fight, but together we can beat this cancer. It will become part of the past. You will be happy to forget it, along with the environment where it started."

"I hope you are right. Y'know that I get a lot of strength from watching you, taking on projects where the odds are against you. And without fear."

"I'll let you in on a little secret. I have never been so scared of anything in my life. But I will force myself to think in a positive manner. I know we will make it through. After all it is you that will be suffering the pain we are facing in the next months," I say, glancing over. "You are the strong one really."

"OK, boss. You are correct. Shut up and drive."

"There you go. That's the Gineen I know and love."

"And if you need help, let me know."

"Nah, it won't take that long. I look forward to checking

in to the inn around lunch time. Roger has taken care of everything. I don't know how we'll ever be able to thank him."

"Dummy, he doesn't need thanks. He really loves us, y'know?"

"I do know," I agree, "but that doesn't stop me from wanting to repay him."

Gineen dismisses me with the flick of her wrist. "Don't worry a second about that; he has all the money he will be able to spend in a lifetime of extravagant living."

"Really?" I ask. "And you know that how?"

"Are you forgetting that I was the only one on the staff of Casino Royale who he trusted? I had access to all the Casino records," she explains. "Besides, he told me the one thing he regretted in life was that he had worked so hard and never had a family. I always suspected that he had some sort of a thwarted love life in his past that he wouldn't talk about. Just a suspicion, mind you, but a woman has a feel for this kind of thing."

"I just hope we will see him soon." I slow the car to a stop and then turn. "So that I can thank him properly for everything he's done for us. Without him, I'd still be chasing errant husbands in New Haven. I never would have met you at the Casino."

"I fully expect to see him in Boston soon. It will take him some time to replace the gang of Casino thieves with people he can trust. With all the gang rotting away in the Tribal Prison for years, it should serve as a reminder to anyone else who has any vision of making off with a penny of the Casino's cash. But I know he will come to visit as soon as things calm down. My instinct tells me we also may see your old friend Sally Langone from the Connecticut DMV. I noticed that they caught on to each other at our wedding."

Sally is a clerk who developed a sideline helping track down people by using the state's license apparatus. She helped me more than once.

After about an hour, Gineen falls sound asleep, with her head on my shoulder. She didn't wake up until we reached the Inn. We chose this Inn because it was just minutes from the Dana Farber where Gineen will have her treatment. As she awakes, she has a puzzled look on her beautiful face for a moment. Then her eyes blink, and she has a questioning look on her face.

"Is this where we're staying?" she asks. "It looks so elegant."

"It is elegant and small, but so close to Dana Farber."

"Is this more of Roger's doing? It looks so expensive."

"It is. So, relax and enjoy it," I say. "We have a hard time facing us. We will need all the luxury we can get for a while. Besides, you just got finished telling me he had much more money than he needs. Speaking of that, suppose we just lay around all afternoon and watch movies and eat? After all, we have a week or so before your treatment begins, so there is no immediate pressure."

"Stop trying to baby me, will you? I know you don't want to do that and neither do I. So, let's have lunch and do some exploring of this great big city which neither of us has ever seen before."

"I'm not trying to baby you," I say. "Well, maybe a little. But subconsciously. Let's go eat."

We have a great lunch in the Inn's dining room. After I sign the check with my room number I realize that it, too, will be paid by Roger. I feel another small twinge of guilt.

"Would you like to walk or take the car?" I ask.

"Not much exercising in riding around in a car," she says. "Old man."

"OK, we walk. Shall we ask the bell captain where the sights are?"

"Nah. Let's just wander for a while."

We walk out onto Longwood Avenue and stand there looking each way for a moment. Directly across the street is a group of gray imposing buildings which I know to be the campus of Harvard Medical School. Not much of an attraction for tourists. I once worked there four years on a study of Fatal Highway Collisions. To our left a few blocks away is the intersection with Huntington Avenue.

"Look," Gineen says, "I see some green over there to our right. Let's go look."

We walk a couple of blocks in that direction and see a beautiful swath of green with a stream in the middle.

"Gineen, this is part of Frederick Law Olmsted's famous Emerald Necklace," I explain. "He was a famous designer who started this project in 1878 with the intention of linking several of the city's existing parks and, at the same time, cleaning up some of the swampy areas along the way. That stream in the middle is the Muddy River and the town of Brookline is just on the other side. Let's cross the street, and walk down the river on one of the paths parallel to the river. Lots of traffic on the Riverway, so hold my hand and be careful. Lots of traffic on the Riverway. Boston drivers are known the world over their recklessness and disregard for the other guy either driving another car, or walking."

We make it across the street without incident and walk into the park.

"My husband is so smart and knows everything," she says.

"I thought you had never been here."

"When I was detecting way back in New Haven, before I went to the Casino, I had plenty of time waiting for the errant husbands and wives to finish their lovemaking, so I could snap their picture leaving the motel or apartment. Without something to read, I would have gone batty. I absorbed a lot of minutiae. This park was especially interesting to me because it is relatively close to Fenway Park."

"How neat. My daddy is a long time Red Sox fan. Let's go there so you can take my picture in front of Fenway Park. You have a camera with you?

"My new smart phone has a camera. It was a wedding present from a few friends. I have barely used it, but I probably can figure it out. Fenway is a bit of a walk. You do know that the start of the baseball season is a couple of weeks away, so Fenway is closed."

"You know everything. I'm so lucky."

"You are... OUCH! What was that punch for?"

"To remind you to get a handle on your conceit."

"You said it, I didn't – "

"OUCH!!"

Another one. I don't bother to ask. We walk out of the park and over to Brookline Avenue. I have all I could do to keep up with her. The cancer has not affected her strength at all. I shudder to think what the treatments will do to her. We find a souvenir shop open on Yawkey Way, where I buy her a Red Sox cap and take a bunch of photos of her. She pretends she is a player.

"Hey, it's getting close to dinnertime," I point out. "Let's grab a ride back to the inn."

"What do you mean a ride back?"

"See those colored cars over there? They are called taxicabs," I say sarcastically. "Surely, you've seen one of them before."

"Don't call me Shirley, and you're cruising for another bruise if you keep that up," she says. "I happen to know that cabs cost money. We have four good legs so why waste the money?"

"Because it's late, I'm tired, and we have half a million dollars in the bank. To say nothing of the house we got for a wedding present, which is worth at least that much."

"You put it that way," she says, "call one over."

I flag one down. As I slip into the backseat, I ask, "Would you take us to the inn at Longwood Medical, please?"

"Sure. My name is Sam Jones," he says. After we settle in the back seat, Sam turns and asks, "If you don't mind my asking were you shopping for tickets to the Red Sox opening day?"

"No. We know that we would not have a chance of finding any of those. Everyone in the Boston Metro Area wants to be there on opening day."

"You're right about that," he says slyly. "But I know someone who might be able to fix you up with a couple of bleacher seats. Let me give you a card. Call me if you are interested."

"By all means. We could very well be interested. April 3rd is not very far away."

Gineen looks at me like I was crazy.

"April 3rd is more than a week away. I will have started my treatment by then," she says.

"So, what?" I ask. "A few hours in the sun will be good for you."

"Provided I'm not throwing up every five minutes."

"You'll be fine. I guarantee it."

I probably have just stuck my foot in my mouth and wish immediately that I had not said that. I see the expression on the face of the cab driver darken in the rear-view mirror.

"Sorry. I didn't realize you were a patient there. Please, I'll get two tickets and they will be on me. Just give me a call and I will drop them off at the inn. Give me your name, so I will know how to get them to you. My wife had a bad case of breast cancer five years ago. The doctors and nurses and the entire staff there are the best. She came through the ordeal just fine. She has been free of any sign of a return ever since. You are going to a great place. I know you will be fine."

"That's so kind of you Mr. Jones," I say, "but we can pay for the tickets."

"I wouldn't hear of it. If I am working that day, I hope you will call me for a ride to the park."

I swear I hear a small quiver in his voice and see tears forming in his eyes. Gineen leans over the seat and says to him, "We will gladly accept your kind offer, but only on the condition that you and your wife be our guests for dinner when I am recovered."

"That's a deal. Here's a card. Just call me at that number if you need any more rides. It's my home phone. Be sure you don't call the dispatcher because someone else is likely to get the call. Here we are. You have a good afternoon and evening."

We get out of the cab and he drives away without collecting the fare. I put my arm around her shoulders as we enter the lobby.

"Amazing. Is it not?" I say. "This is a good omen, don't you agree? We leave one Jones in Voluntown and pick up a new one hours after we arrive. A good sign, I think."

"I hope so. Let's have some lunch. Since we're already here. Is it OK if we just eat here? We can talk about dinner while we eat lunch."

"OK," I agree, "but tonight we are having dinner in the Back Bay at the restaurant of your choice.

"You are so sweet," she says, "but it's OK to eat here."

"We will be doing a lot of that in the next few months. Let's get out while we can."

"You are a sweetheart and I'll go anywhere with you. How about Italian?" Gineen suggests. "I seem to remember there are some good ones in this city, and the North End.

"I'll check with the desk later," I say as we head to lunch.

I call down and they recommend a place called Sorellina. We decide not to bother our driver of this morning and instead call a cab which takes us there in ten minutes

"Oh my, Patrick. What a lovely place," she says as we step out of the cab.

"Yes, isn't it?" I agree. "This is Copley Square and that building across the street is the famous Boston Public Library. It was founded in 1852. It is as beautiful inside as it is outside. One day we'll have to come back here and tour the inside. They have more than 1.7 million rare books as well as prints, photographs, post cards, maps and many important collections. One of them is a collection of extremely rare posters commissioned by something called the Boston Public Safety Committee. It was founded by a group of wealthy citizens to encourage the U.S. to get into World War I."

"Aren't you a fountain of knowledge that just keeps

spouting?"

"I confess that I have been cheating," I admit. "The computer along with the help of Wikipedia can really make a country dummy like me seem so erudite."

"When will you ever drop that phony dummy role?" she asks, rolling her eyes. "You are one smart dude and I hate it when you play dumb."

"Hey, I have an awful lot to learn, so sometimes I really feel quite ignorant," I say, dropping my eyes to my feet. "Just look how I messed up my life with my first wife Sheila and the two kids, Cynthia and Mark."

"For your information millions of Americans get divorced. Some very smart people are outright dumb when it comes to picking a mate," she points out. "Time that you stopped beating yourself up. Or do you still love her?"

"Once upon a time yes. But it's all gone now. There is only one woman in the world that I love dearly. I'm looking at her. Get used to the idea. Now get into that restaurant. Let's see what they have to offer to assuage the hunger of two love birds from the country."

The maître d' finds us a table. The place is only half full. I suppose that is because of the early hour. When we are seated, I open the menu to find a very elaborate list of meals. Imagine ordering from such an erudite menu at this early hour.

"We are the only country bumkins here," I joke.

"Correct, sweet bumpkin. Do you want me to order for you?"

"Absolutely. But no Carpaccio. I don't eat Venison loin or any other loin for that matter. And please, no Foie Gras."

When the waiter comes for our order and Gineen starts

to order, he gives me a look that would have made President Trump shrink into the floor. I'm thinking he gets no tip if I have any say in the matter, which I know I will not. I figure he has no respect for a guy who lets his wife do the ordering.

"We'll start with a bottle of Burgundy wine and the Arugula Insalata. We will follow that with two orders of oysters and then we'll talk about the main dish," Gineen says to him.

"Thank you, ma'am. Good choices." Another look of sheer disdain as he turns and leaves for the kitchen.

"I believe he figured out that I am not a Boston Brahmin. Don't you?"

"We both can be thankful that you are not," I say. "Don't be so sensitive. Your Irish roots are obvious, and they apparently are still not very welcome by the Brahmins in this town or those who serve them. By the way, did you know that oysters tend to increase sexual activity?"

"Then perhaps we should order another round."

"I don't think you need *ANY* oysters!"

The waiter returns with said oysters and salad, and a sweet smile for Gineen. One more sneer for me.

"If I walk out of this place without decking that guy, I should get a Nobel Peace Prize."

"Yep. I'll submit you name. No doubt you will be a shoo-in."

The oysters and the salad are great, but I would have preferred a Budweiser over the wine. Nevertheless, I mark this place down in my brain for at least one more visit.

"For the main course I'm going to order salmon for me and tuna for you. We can share."

"It's a deal boss, but let me order when he comes back.

Really shake him up. Maybe he'll smile at me and scowl at you."

"I don't think so, but let's try it."

A few minutes later he shows up. He asks Gineen, "Have you decided on your main course?"

"No, she hasn't but I have. Tuna for me and Salmon for the lady. Oh, and bring me a Budweiser, would you?"

He glares at me for a moment, and says, "Yes, sir. Your order will be ready in a few minutes."

"Thank you."

He must have realized that I am the one with the wallet who will pay his tip because he is back quickly with my beer and then our fish ten minutes later. The meal is terrific and offsets my travails with the damn waiter.

Next morning at breakfast, Gineen opens the conversation with, "Are you up for some exercise this morning, my big handsome husband? It's been less than a week since we were married and I'm still not tired of you, but I want you to keep fit, so we need a replacement for Mt. Misery and our cycling."

"Well thanks for the vote of confidence," I say. "I guess that I should enter the first husband of the year contest that comes along. It's my charm, no doubt."

"Nah. It's more the size of your love instrument and your skill at using it. I'm sure I won't get tired of you for at least another week. That's assuming you pay attention to your primary job. In fact, your only job."

"All this flattery will go right to my head. Please, no more. Suppose we get to the exercise. My research says there are some good jogging paths on the Charles River Esplanade. It sounds like a delightful place to run."

"And where is this place?"

"As you might have guessed, it runs along the Charles River which separates Boston and Cambridge. It's also the home of the Hatch Memorial Shell where they have concerts, movies, and fireworks on July 4th. You can learn to sail on the Charles. Sounds like a dandy place to jog. Better than Mount Misery back in Voluntown."

"Great. What are we waiting for? Can we walk there?"

"Too far for that. Can't drive because it will be difficult. We best take a taxi. The Esplanade is separated from the Back Bay by Storrow Drive, a multi-lane expressway. There are pedestrian overpasses at several locations."

"Are you sure that Daniel Law Olmstead wasn't your great grandad? You have done a marvelous job on this research. Sounds suspiciously like something out of Wikipedia."

"What if it is? I'm going down to the Concierge and I'll have him call our Mr. Jones. C'mon."

He calls Mr. Jones, and a few minutes later Jones shows up.

"Nice to see you again, Sam," he says. "Can you take us to the Hatch Shell overpass on Arlington?"

"Oh sure. I take my kids down there on the weekends to sail their tiny sailboats in the lagoon. You must be going jogging."

"We are," I admit. "My little boy pants must have tipped you off."

"They did. Jogging is something I don't do, but probably should," he says. "Too much sitting on my can in this cab."

He slows down to a stop as the Hatch Shell comes into view. "Here we are. I'll just double park for a moment here on

Beacon Street."

"Seems to be an epidemic of that in this town," I joke. "Thanks for the ride, Sam. Keep the change."

"Thank you, sir. Have a good run. Call me if you need a ride back to the inn."

"Thanks again, Sam," I say, waving him goodbye. "We will do that."

We climb the stairs to the pedestrian overpass and land just west of the Hatch Shell, just along the Drive on one side and the river on the other. Storrow Drive is a roaring four-lane expressway mostly depressed below grade. This point would be about halfway along the Esplanade.

"Why don't we head that way to the west? That way we get to pass the lagoon, see MIT across the Charles and the rear of some lovely Back Bay apartment buildings on the other side of Storrow Drive. C'mon and remember, wifey, this is not a race. I see you are up to your old tricks," I say as she starts to turn on the heat.

"Big baby," she says between breaths. "A little racing never hurt anyone."

"C'mon. There are lots of things to see. Take it easy. This is all new."

We set out for the MIT bridge at a moderate pace. When we arrive, we stop at the bridge and turn around and head back toward the Hatch. The view there is better, and it's a bit farther away from the noise of Storrow Drive.

"Look at those apartment buildings across Storrow. What a grand place that would be to live," I say. "Holy mackerel, some of them even have an outdoor patio with a small garden."

"Holy mackerel? Is this the speech of an experienced and

sophisticated administrator? Let's go back and see if we can make it all the way to the other end of the trail at the Museum of Science."

"So, I see that you have been doing a little research of your own."

We slow as we pass the lagoon to watch some of the youngsters sail their toy boats. Gineen stops and I see tears forming in her eyes.

"What is it?" I ask.

"I guess I was thinking about our starting a family and now having to postpone it."

"I know that." I hug her for a moment and feel a gentle sob.

"We'll have all the babies you can handle and soon," I say. "At least as many for a basketball team. Now increase the pace a bit and head for the Museum of Science."

We don't exactly race but we are close to it, and make it to the Museum in no time at all.

"Want to go in and look around?" I offer.

Gineen shakes her head. "Nah, save it for another time when you are wearing your big boy pants."

We stop and admire the Hatch Shell, imagining Arthur Fiedler conducting the Boston Pops here.

"Y'know, I'm going to enjoy our stay here. Maybe we will end up living in this area for good."

"I'd like that too. Let's go on back to the Inn, change our clothes, and find a dandy place to eat. I'm starving."

"Again?"

It takes me ten minutes to wash up and change my clothes and twenty minutes later Gineen is also done. At least, this gives me time to explore the internet and find a restaurant.

When she's ready, Gineen exits the bathroom in a lovely dress.

"My, don't you look beautiful?" I say.

"But you're only saying that because it's true," she asks, "right?"

"Couldn't be any truer. Now that we've got that out of the way, let's go get a cab."

"You mind telling me where we are going or is it a secret?"

"No secret but I don't want you to be put off by the name. It's in the downtown area. Called Sweet Cheeks. I'm not kidding either. It gets good reviews."

"Sounds like a drive-in, out in the boonies, or a strip club. Is this a variation on Hooters, where the boobs and cheeks are hanging out?"

"I don't think so but we'll find out when there."

Find out, we did.

"Damn," I joke, "no waitresses with anything hanging out."

"Would you like me to find a Hooters?" Gineen asks with a smirk.

"Nah, I'm too hungry."

The place is like an old-fashioned cafeteria/deli where you take a tray up to the serving counter and load up with food and drink.

"The food looks delicious and you don't have to depend on anyone to determine what the proper size of a serving is."

"It does look good. We stay. No Hooters, but try real hard to control yourself, piggy."

I load up a tray with something called Heritage Breed Pulled Pork, potato salad, and coleslaw. Gineen follows me with natural pulled chicken and black-eyed peas.

When we sit down at a table, she eyes my plate with a tinge of disgust in her eyes. "I suppose I don't need to ask if you intend to eat all of that, do I?"

"This is good for openers but when I go back for a second-round I will get smaller portions."

"That's good for Sweet Cheeks, or else they might run out of a week's supply of pulled pork."

"You're not insinuating that I eat too much, are you?"

"Not insinuating anything. I already know that you eat too much." Gineen takes a bite of her food. "Yum, this chicken is delicious. Congratulations, you picked a winner. I don't know if they deliver but if they do, we'll order some when I get into my treatment."

I reach for her hand across the table. "You are a bit scared about the process staring you in the face," I say, "aren't you?"

"Wouldn't you be?"

"Sure. Maybe it won't be as bad as you think it will."

"From your lips. Will you still love me when my hair falls out?"

"Don't even think about that and of course I will still love you. If you're finished, I am going after dessert. How does a Banana Mess sound?"

"Sounds good for you but I'll settle for plain old butterscotch pudding."

We were relatively silent during our desserts until she looked me in the eye and said, "Patrick, you need to promise me something. Don't answer me now but just think about it for a while. OK?"

"Sure," I say and put down my spoon.

"Even if my treatment goes well, it's going to be three

hard months, maybe more. I don't expect you to hang around holding my hand."

I start to interrupt, but she holds up her hand to stop me.

"You promised to listen," she says. "I started to say, I don't expect you to hang around all that time. Nor do I even want you to. That would be boring for both of us."

"Are you saying that I bore you?"

"No. It's just that hanging around the house is not what you do! I don't want to watch you go berserk. What I am saying is that I want you to do what you do best. Find a detective job. Whatever kind of a detecting job you find is likely to need erratic hours of your time and that might work to our advantage. But in any event, go to work!"

"I promise to think about it," I say and resume eating my dessert. "There's enough crime in and around Boston, so I expect there to be no shortage of work."

She grabbs my hand and squeezes; I realize how important it is to her.

"Enough of this talk, sweet cheeks," she says. "What have you planned for this afternoon?"

"Well, nothing, but suppose we improvise. We are right in the most active theatre district, north of New York, so why don't we wander around and make a little list for future reference."

"Great. I hardly have seen any live theatre in my life so that's very exciting."

We start our tour at the Paramount Center which was built in 1932 for movies of the talking variety.

"Gineen, this is an old movie theatre that has been restored into two separate performing areas by Emerson College," I explain. "The exterior is great and reminds me of those old elegant movie theaters of the 1930s and 40s. The Toshiba says there is nothing scheduled just now so we'll have to wait a while to see what the inside looks like."

"It looks so elegant that it would be fun just to watch a movie in it."

"Yep. I think we will skip the next one on my list. It's the Chamber Theatre which looks like it produces educational shows mostly for children. We'll bring our kids here when they are old enough. Are you tired? We could stop now and head back to the inn."

"I won't tell you again. Stop trying to baby me!" Gineen exclaims. "When I'm tired, I'll let you know."

"OK, then it's off to the Wilbur Theatre, which is a landmark in the theatre scene."

When we get there, we discover that they are advertising music and stand-up comedy shows. Not what I expected. The CTI Emerson Colonial Theatre has nothing showing.

"I'm starting get a bit disappointed in Boston," Gineen admits. "There must be some legitimate theatre somewhere in town. I've seen enough for today's culture tour. I'm tired. Let's head back to the Inn."

"Sure," I agree.

"I'm going to call our favorite cab driver, Sam Jones, and see if he can pick us up."

Jones answers on the second ring. Tells me he can pick us up in ten minutes. He does arrive in ten minutes. Naturally he gets rewarded with another fat tip. I think we have a friend for life. And not just because of the tips we gave him. Just because he rather likes talking to us. We have dinner at the inn. When we finish, I am ready to go up to our suite when Gineen grabs my arm and tells me in no uncertain terms that she needs some real culture after all that walking this afternoon.

"The concierge gave me the number of the Coolidge Corner Cinema," she says. "We are going there to see a movie called *A Sense of Ending*. A real live movie in a real live theatre. What do you say?"

"I'd rather see *The Godfather*, but I'll go along to get along."

"Humph. I'm sure I can find someone to accompany me if it's such a strain for you."

"Just kidding. You call Sam."

She does, and I'll be dammed if he doesn't pop right over and drive us the very short distance over to the theatre in Brookline.

"Y'all go in and check the time when the movie is over, so I can pick you up. It'd be hard to find a cab at the late hour over here."

He comes back at 10:45 and drives us back to the inn.

"Call me in the morning if you need a ride anywhere," he offers. "It's my day off so I am available anytime."

On the way up to our room I say to Gineen, "It's nice to have your own car and driver. You know, it's weird but I have this feeling that I am about to get him into trouble, or that someone is watching us. Probably just a holdover reaction from the Casino Royale's experiences."

"Just your over worked imagination, I'm sure."

"Sam's a big boy and can take care of himself. Not your concern. I'm sure he knows what he's doing," I say, trying to reassure myself. "Besides our big fat tips are starting to add up."

"I guess you're right and I really do like him. Old man, do you think you have enough energy to love me proper?"

"You just watch."

"I intend to do just that."

It is 1 a.m. before we slid off to sleep. Next morning, at breakfast I look at my luscious wife and say to her, "You know, I've been thinking a lot about what you said last night."

"You mean when I was in the throes of mad passionate love? Oh, goodness what did I say?"

"Well no, I mean about finding work. You wouldn't really hate me if I hung around the house and didn't look for work. Would you?'

"Of course, I wouldn't hate you," she says, "but if you sit by my side for three months, will it help me recover? I think not. I'd worry constantly about your mental state. The reality is that you might end up hating me for taking you out of the normal patterns of your life. Don't say anything," she says, as I started to interrupt her. "Maybe hate is too strong a word but I can see how you would resent me, at least. I don't want to risk that. Time is the best healer and if I don't make it through this ordeal, I at least want to know that you will find happiness again and you never resented me."

"Nonsense," I almost shout. "Don't even think like that. You will make it. We will be making babies before too long."

"Ahh, the power of positive thinking. I'll go along with that. Now, all that is beside the point. The point is find some work for you, remember?"

"Maybe there's a job here in the Inn," I suggest, half joking. "Waiter, or janitor or something like that."

"That's not very funny. By the time my treatment starts, I'll be living in a house, remember?" she says. "On second thought, it is funny, picturing you trying to balance a tray of food and getting it to a table without spilling everything over some valued guests of the Inn. You know what I meant when I said work. In case you have forgotten what you do best, I'll remind you that you are the world's second-best detective."

"Oh really, and who might be the best?"

"Sherlock Holmes, dummy."

"You mean I lost the contest to a dead man?" I joke. "I will call Roger. See if he knows what's going on around this big city."

"Good idea. Don't put it off, do it right now."

"You are one tough cookie. OK, boss. Right now."

As directed, I pick up the phone and dial Roger's number. I hold while they find him.

"Roger Jones here," he says on the other end.

"Hi Roger," I say. "Patrick on this end of the line in the grand city of Boston. How goes everything?"

"Very well," he says, his voice perking up. "You wouldn't believe how smoothly things are going now that the gang is in jail. To say nothing of the increases in daily revenues, thanks to you and your good work. We've already covered your fee and then some." He pauses, dropping his cheery attitude. "Is Gineen OK? Have they started her treatment yet?"

"My good work? I seem to remember that I got a little help from you and Gineen," I say. "And, no, her treatment has not started. She has an appointment in a couple of days for an interview and the actual treatment won't be scheduled until early next week depending on the results of Friday's examination. We have done nothing except eat, sleep, and walk.

"The real reason I called you is about work," I admit.

"Gineen and I have decided that I should go to work, instead of moping around here for three or four months. While I could do some advertising to find something reasonable, that would take some time. We thought perhaps, with your contacts, you might provide us with some promising leads."

"I certainly can do that. I'll make a few calls to friends in a couple of insurance companies and see what's going on. By the way, I gave your name to a real estate broker just this morning. She should be getting in touch with you very soon. She mentioned two houses located within walking distance of Dana Farber that seemed to be reasonably priced. I purposely did not tell her that I was picking up the tab as I promised you I would. I figured that would have resulted in a substantial increase in the price. So, use your powers of negotiation with her to get the best price you can. Once you do that you can tell her that I am buying it for a wedding present for two of the finest people in the world. I guess you already know that I feel you two are the children that I never was lucky enough to have. Give Gineen a big hug and a kiss and tell her that I will be up there to see you before very long. Now that I have a trustworthy assistant manager who knows the Casino inside and out, I have the flexibility to get away once in a while. Bye for now."

"Bye Roger and thanks."

I reach over and give Gineen a monster hug and a kiss. "That's from Roger. This one's from me," I say and kiss her again. "He is amazing. Not only is he going to call some of his insurance company buddies to see if they might have a project worthy of my talents, but he also has called a real estate broker who already has two houses for us to look at. That's the wedding present he promised us. I know that we both did some good work in rounding up the mob that was hurting Casino Royale, but he has paid us for that many times over.

"I know. It's sad in a way. I have put his name on the list of things I want to do to take my mind off this ordeal."

"He already has something to do, manage the casino. What he doesn't have is someone to love nor anything to look forward to. I intend to fix that."

"You really think you are capable of doing that?"

"I found you. Didn't I?"

"That's funny, I thought I found you, babe."

"That's what I wanted you to think ever since we met at that restaurant in Norwich where I used to work."

"You mean the G Bar?"

"A lot of water over the dam since I lured you into a trap there."

"Since we are on the subject," Gineen says, "I have a feeling that anything you might do about finding Roger a playmate might be wasted effort."

"What do you mean?" I ask.

"Well I saw his eyes light up when we introduced him to Sally Langone at our wedding in his suite," she explains. "I wouldn't be a bit surprised if she latched onto him. Or vice versa."

"I guess I missed that. Maybe, I'll scout around for a backup just in case. Are you ready for some strenuous exercise, a run or a walk? Or maybe both, big baby. Walk all the way down to the overpass onto the Esplanade and then jog back here as far as we can go and then more walking."

"That's a long haul even for people who have done this kind of exercise routine for years," Gineen admits.

"This mean you are weaseling out?"

"Who me?" she asks. "Of course not."

"Good, I need you to navigate. My personal Garmin."

"It makes me feel so good to be compared to a machine. OK, out the door and make a right turn onto Longwood Avenue and then another right turn onto Brookline Avenue. We follow that all the way to Kenmore Square where we pick up Beacon Street. We follow that all the way to the Hatch Shell Overpass onto the Esplanade. "

"Do you want to walk or jog to the Overpass?"

"How about a power walk. Save some energy for the run on the Esplanade."

"You go. I'll follow right on your tail."

"Ooh. How nice for you."

We power walk all the way to Kenmore Square, but she starts to slow down a bit farther on. We continue to get questioning looks from the other pedestrians on Beacon, most of them wearing business clothes or stylish dress. Some of them, no doubt, on shopping trips to the glamorous shops on Marlborough and Arlington Streets.

"Don't make fun of me. I'm just saving energy for the jog along the Esplanade and all the way back to the inn, where I will arrive about fifteen minutes before you, unless you give up and call Sam Jones to drive you back."

She starts to pull away, but I paced myself, saving fuel for the last half of the run. It doesn't work. By the time we get off The Esplanade and over to Brookline Avenue, I am pooped but she keeps going. When I finally get back to the inn, she is waiting for me on a bench.

"Where you been champ? I've been back for fifteen minutes."

"I would have been right behind you, but I had to stop and assist an elderly pedestrian who was having a heart attack."

"Good story on such short notice. I'd like to eat here at the inn. OK with you?"

We both shuck off our sweaty clothes and shower. I hope we might do a nooner, but she isn't interested, so we dress and go down to the restaurant. As I pass the check-in desk, the clerk tells me I have several messages. He retrieves two messages from our box to open. When we get to a table, I open them.

"Roger's real estate broker has been busy. Both messages are from her. All right with you if I call her to see if we can look at houses this afternoon?"

"Why not?"

"OK. I'll go back to the lobby. Get the messages and her number. Back in a few minutes."

Back in the room, I call her office.

"Good afternoon," greets a receptionist, "Layton Realty."

"Hi. My name is Patrick Ingel and Marcelle has some houses to show my wife and me. Is she available?

"Sure, let me get her for you." I hear the receptionist's heels clink against a hardwood floor. They disappear and reappear. Another voice speaks.

"Hello, Mr. Ingel, this is Marcie Layton. Nice to talk to you. I do have two lovely homes within walking distance of the clinic in Brookline. Are you ready to look at them today?"

"I am," I tell her. "How about after lunch. Can we make it at one?"

"Excellent. I will pick you up at the inn. I know you are going to love both these homes. See you then."

"OK. We will be waiting outside the inn."

As good as her word, Marcie pulls up in a large Cadillac right at one o'clock. We both sit in the front seat. Before she pulls out into traffic, she reaches across and shakes our hands.

"Hi. I'm Marcie, nice to see you," she says, smiling. "You're going to love both these homes. Your only trouble will be picking between them."

It only takes a couple of minutes to make the drive across the Muddy River into Brookline. As soon as she pulls into a driveway, I know this is the one. There would be no need to look any further. The grounds are nicely landscaped and well-tended, and it is a small sparkling house.

"Gineen, say hello to your new home."

"It looks great from the outside," she says skeptically, "but how can you know anything about the inside before you see it?"

"Male intuition."

Marcie opens the door and when we step inside a sharp intake of breath sounds from Gineen.

"It's beautiful," she says, "but all these rooms that we don't really need that many."

"You're right. It is large – 2500 square feet with five bedrooms. Lots of space for entertaining and for guests who might want to stay overnight," adds our friendly broker.

We continue the tour, and I am certain it is the house for us.

"I do have a few units with two bathrooms, but they are further away from the clinic and considerably more expensive. If it doesn't work for you, I have other places you can look at."

"Nah. Don't think so. The others can't be as close to Dana Farber as this is," I say. "Somehow, we must make this one work. What is the asking price for the two units?"

"You mean you would be interested in both?"

"Yes. That's exactly what I mean but only if the price is right."

"But Mr. Jones told me explicitly not to talk price with you."

"He is a nice, well-meaning guy, but the house is for us. Everything depends on getting the property at a sensible price. Why don't you go back to your office and talk to the owners of the property? We'll expect to hear from you by the end of the business day. We would have to take possession immediately. The property is vacant, and it will be a cash deal. No mortgage. I see no reason why the deal can't be done in a few days."

"I don't know if it can be done that quickly but I'll try," Marcie says hesitantly. "What about a title search, that usually takes up to several weeks?"

"We will not insist on a title search. A bank will not be involved because there will be no mortgage on the property. My wife's cancer treatment will likely start early next week, and we'll need some time to furnish at least one of the units. I will pay the owner's legal fees, so long as we don't have to wait. I don't want lazy lawyers getting in the way."

"You seem to have thought of everything," Marcie says with a smile.

"I hope so. But don't forget, we always have the option to stay at the Inn for a while."

Marcelle drops us off at the Inn. It's too early for dinner, so I ask Gineen what she wants to do.

"You know I was thinking yesterday that it would be good for me to have one of those electronic readers," she says.

"You mean a Kindle?" I ask.

"Well yeah. I guess so."

"They are great. You can put a whole bunch of books on them and you can get music too. I'll check with the desk and find out where the nearest Best Buy is."

"They told me the nearest one is in the Arsenal Mall in Watertown. I'll call Sam."

I call and they say he's on a call, but will be finished soon and will come to get us.

Sam shows up twenty minutes later and takes us out to the Arsenal Mall in Watertown, which is a quick fifteen minute drive, west on Storrow Drive. We end up buying two Kindles with cases and then return to the inn.

By now it's time for dinner. Gineen expresses a desire for Italian food in an informal restaurant. Sam takes us to Dillon's Restaurant on Boylston Street. We persuade him to eat with us and then take us back to the inn. Dillon's is a small comfortable restaurant with real Italian food – an enjoyable dinner. Sam proves once again that his intellect is not what you might expect from a cab driver. We laugh all through the meal at stories he tells about some of his experiences in and out of the cab. I tell him he should put these funny stories into a book.

"What? Me? I'm just a cab driver. I don't know how to write a book."

CHAPTER II

"Sure, you do," I argue. "All you need to do is talk into a microphone. Somebody else will do the rest."

"Really?" he asks. "And you think people will buy such a book?"

"I do indeed. Let me know when you will have a day off work, and I will help you get started."

"I will and thanks for dinner. You two are good people." Sam slows to a stop in front of the inn. "Here we are. Please have a good night."

"You too Sam," I say. "We'll see you soon."

As soon as we get out of the cab, Gineen grabs me, throws her arms around me, and plants a big kiss on my cheek.

"What's that for?"

"Just because you are such a kind man, offering to help Sam write a book," she comments. "Every day we are together, I learn a bit more about you."

"Oh shucks. It's nothing."

"What an asshole you are when do that *oh shucks* bit."

After our tiring day, we stay at the Inn and have dinner in their restaurant. We are in bed by nine. Gineen reads a mystery novel on her new Kindle. I watch a Celtics game on the tube. We shut off the lights at eleven and sleep straight through until seven the next morning. Over my corned beef hash and eggs, we talk about today's list of things we plan to do.

"We still have five days before your first examination so let's plan our day today. First, I expect to receive a call from our favorite realtor, Marcelle. I know she will have a proposed purchase price for the house, and we'll want to sit down with her to do some negotiating on the price. And on other not so important details like the closing date. Next, we must go out and buy some basic furniture. We should talk to Roger about these items. I'm shooting to be in our new house by Tuesday or Wednesday of next week."

"I'm excited about getting settled in there but isn't Tuesday or Wednesday impossible?"

"You should know that nothing is impossible where money is concerned," I say. "And, oh yeah, I am pretty good at organizing things."

"Yep, you are. Where do we start?"

"I expect Marcelle to call in the morning, so I want to stay here until she does call. But two of us don't have to hang out here. It would be the best use of our time if you could find a good place to furniture shop. Make a list of the essentials. Try and find one place where you could get it all. That would speed things up. Maybe the desk could provide some leads. Our friendly cab driver can probably help. In fact, skip the desk clerk. What I need is a 60-inch TV set, a desk, a locking file cabinet, and a few lamps. And of course, a king-sized bed."

"Considering that I am likely to be uncomfortable for a few months, it might be wiser to get two twin sized beds and put them together. In the future when we have the children, they will be able to use them. Then we could buy a king for us."

"I don't much like that idea but you do whichever you think is the best option. That goes for the kitchen, too. Just make sure the fridge is large enough for a case of Bud. Furniture stores are notorious for taking forever to buy the stuff you want, so make sure the items are in stock and they can deliver it fast. A few extra bucks can sometimes speed things up."

"Seems like you had this all planned out."

"Well I told you that I am a good organizer. See you when you get back."

Thirty minutes after she left with Sam, the telephone rings. I answer cheerily, "Good morning."

"Good morning, Mister Ingel. Can we sit down this morning and go over the details on the sale of the Brookline property?"

"Of course, where would you like to meet and what time?" I ask.

"Best if we went over it here in my office. Could you make it by ten?"

"I'll be there."

On the dot of ten, I walk into her reception area, where the receptionist greets me warmly.

"Mr. Ingel, please have a seat," she says. "Marcelle is expecting you. She is on the phone but will be finished in a few minutes."

I venture to say that the telephone call was a tiny trick intended to show me how busy she is. I play along. It is a full ten minutes before the receptionist leads me into Marcelle's private office.

"Good morning, Patrick. Have a seat. Sorry you had to

wait so long but the call I was on was very important and I couldn't put it off."

"I understand what you are saying." I really did understand; there was no call at all, I thought to myself.

"I met with owners of the Longwood Avenue property late yesterday. I spent some time with them trying to convince them that you really wanted the property and probably weren't going to accept an offer under their asking price."

"And that price is what?"

"Seven and a half million. It took me a long time to convince them that the property would not sell at that price, at least not in the foreseeable future. They finally relented and agreed to reduce the asking price to $7,250,000."

"Good job, Marcelle, but that is still too much for me to handle. So, thank you for your work."

As I stand up as if to leave, she gives me an exasperated look and says, "Hold on. Let me give it one more shot with the owner. Why don't you wait for me in the reception area?"

I am positive this is theatre and doubt there is any call at all. She calls me back into her office after a ten-minute wait.

"You are in luck. It wasn't easy, but they finally agreed to a flat seven million but that's it. They won't budge another penny."

"OK, I think we have a deal, but I need to talk this over with Gineen. I'll be back to you by the end of the day."

Of course, it wasn't Gineen that I called when I got back to the inn but Roger.

"Good morning, Roger," I say, "it's Patrick."

"Good morning to you. What's happening?"

"Well on the Longwood property, the owners have lowered the asking price to seven million for both units. It took two tries. I hesitated to twist anymore because I sensed that was it. They have also agreed to a fast closing, which will be early next week."

"I trust your judgement on the price," he agrees. "How is Gineen getting along?"

"She's fine. Her first appointment is in four days. Just now, she is out looking for some furniture for the unit we will live in."

"You have done your usual fine job. I will wire the money to a bank in Boston. I'll let you know the name of the bank when I make the wire transfer. It should be there this afternoon. One more thing. I have made inquiries to a couple of Insurance companies up there that are owned by the Tribal Council. One of their customers filed an enormous claim just within the past few days. They have not paid it, of course. I will set up an appointment with the president of one of the companies. You will be hearing from him very soon. Solving this theft should be right up your alley."

"Thanks. I can't tell you how much we appreciate all that you have done for us."

"Nonsense. Before this is over, you will have earned every penny that you get. Trust me."

"If there is one person in the world that I would trust with my life, it would be you. Are you planning to come up anytime soon?"

"Yes, but I do not know exactly when," he explains. "Do me a small favor, would you?"

"Anything."

"When I do come up, I'd like to stay in the second unit of the duplex, but I'll need some basic furniture. A bed, a desk, a fridge and whatever else I might need to be comfortable. The name of the insurance company is American Independence and the president is Timothy Allen. They are eager to start this investigation, so expect a call in a day or two. A lot happening, are you OK?"

"I'm fine and actually looking forward to starting work," I admit.

"Good. You take care. Give Gineen a big hug and kiss for me. By the way, when I do come it will only be for a couple of weeks and I expect to bring Sally Langone with me. Another job you did very well. Bye now."

"Bye."

I get right on the phone and call Allen.

"American Independence," the receptionist greets. "How may I direct your call?"

"Good morning. My name is Patrick Ingel. I'm a private investigator and have been asked to talk to Mr. Allen."

"May I tell him what it is about?"

"Until I talk to him, I'd rather keep my call confidential. I have been referred to him by Roger Jones of the Casino Royale in Connecticut. Mr. Allen is expecting my call."

"Certainly, let me get him for you."

"Thanks." I wait a few moments before another voice picks up on the other end of the line.

"Good morning Mr. Ingel," Mr. Allen greets. "Roger Jones has told me all about you. He thinks the world of you, both professionally and personally. Is there a chance you can stop by the office in the next few days? I know why you are in town. I don't want to interfere with your wife's treatment."

"That's quite alright. Her actual treatment does not start until next Monday and we have agreed that it would be best for both of us if I find a job. That gives us four days to talk. By the way, please call me Patrick. If it's OK with you, I would prefer to talk to you outside your office. It's simply that I'd like to be as anonymous as possible until I get the lay of the land, so to speak."

"That's not a problem for me and staying out of the limelight does seem like a good idea. Could you meet me for lunch this afternoon?"

"I could do that. Anyplace that is convenient for you."

"How about Jacob Wirth's restaurant. It's downtown on Stuart Street. We are not apt to meet anyone from the office there during the lunch hour. Does 12:30 work for you?"

"Yes, it does."

"Fine. I'll get there a bit earlier and find a table. Just ask the head waiter for me."

"Great. See you there."

Gineen comes back just before lunch. I meet her at the door and give her a big hug and a kiss on the cheek.

"That one is from Roger. This one is from me," I say as I kiss her sweet lips.

"No more kissing on an empty stomach, buster. All that furniture hunting sapped my strength. Where are we going?"

"Well, I just made a lunch appointment with the head of American Independence Insurance and I am meeting him downtown at 12:30. Want to come along?"

"No. I think you should do that on your own. I would just be a distraction."

"Not to me you wouldn't. Besides you might have some good advice on how to proceed with this investigation, provided that I go ahead with it."

"No. I'll eat here at the Inn and think about where to put

the furniture I bought. It will also give me time to make some lists of all the little things we will need. Groceries and stuff like that. Wait until you see the furniture I bought. It's great and it will all be delivered tomorrow or the day after. I can't wait to move in."

I don't believe I have ever seen anyone so excited about furniture. I think she is moving ahead to the time when we can start a family and live a mostly "normal" life. My makeup is different than hers, so I am content to limit my thoughts all the way into next week. It is good to see her in such a happy mood. Back at the Inn, I prepare a detailed list of all the things that need to be done to make the condo into a real-life home. It is a bloody long list. Such things as getting the utilities changed to our name, putting our name on the mailbox, getting a subscription to the Boston Globe. On and on. Then I call Sam Jones and tell him to pick me up at noontime.

I catch Gineen at the desk furiously making her lists and nuzzle her ear.

"Um, you suppose we could have a nooner at eleven o'clock?"

"I thought you'd never ask. I believe I can work you in between the grocery list and the utensil list. Have your girl call my girl."

"My girl says I'm in. Good of you to see it my way."

Our lovemaking is short and sweet, interrupted by a call from downstairs announcing that Sam Jones awaits.

"Later, sweet love."

"If I'm not here when you get back, it will be because I decided to take a walk. By the way, I have added bicycles to my list."

"Hey, this is not Voluntown. It might be hard to find a place where we would be protected from the curse of Boston drivers."

"I thought of that and there are some places, like along the Fenway and on the Esplanade."

"Let's check that out before we invest in bikes."

"Sure, spoil sport."

"See you later."

I leave her to her lists and meet Sam downstairs.

"Hello Sam. I have a lunch meeting at Jack Wirth's. I assume you know how to get there."

"Of course, I do. Have you there is just a few minutes now that rush hour is not a problem. Everything going well with you?"

"Everything is good. In fact, I have an interview for a possible job. I'm meeting the prospective client at Wirth's."

"Terrific. I may have lunch nearby and then take you home when you are finished. Call me."

"I will."

Inside Wirth's I ask for Mr. Allen and am led to his table.

"Mr. Allen, Patrick Ingel. Nice to meet you."

"If we are to work together you must know that I only respond to Allen."

With that he signals the waiter over and we both order. He orders beer battered mozzarella sticks, and steamed bratwurst with a dark beer. I am about to stick with a cheeseburger when he spots my lack of understanding the menu.

"Why don't you let me order for you?"

"Sure, go ahead."

After he places the order and the waiter leaves, we start to talk about his problem.

"Patrick, here's the story. We have a client, by the name of Brandt, who has recently filed a very large claim with the company. If we can believe him, a small fortune in jewelry has been stolen from his home out in Lincoln, Mass. According to him, there was a break-in the evening when neither his wife nor he were there. One of their servants, a butler, was there but apparently, he sleeps on the third floor where he would be in a poor location to hear anything on the second or first floors. The alleged robbery was reported to the police the next morning when they awoke."

"Let me interrupt you for a moment, if you don't mind."

"No, go right ahead, whenever you want. Feel free to make notes as we go along or even record our conversation. I have a copy of the claim from the client but as of now we have only had a brief contact with the police department. I assume, if you take on the case, you will want to contact the police department yourself."

"Might I ask why you want to hire me? I'm sure that you must have your own in-house investigators."

"Yes, we do. I have several reasons for asking you aboard. First, you've had such a grand success solving the Casino Royale theft. Roger has spoken very highly of you. Second, I've decided that the smaller the investigation staff is, the better. What I am worried about is tipping our hand to the thieves with a mess of routine reports floating around. If you do agree to take on the job, I would like you to work directly with me and keep our involvement with others to an absolute minimum."

"That would be a good approach based on my limited experience with large thefts. If you are following someone, it is better that he knows as little as possible about what you are doing and where you are going. I sense that you have substantial doubts about your clients," I point out. "Yes?"

"I do. Doubt might be too strong a word at this point. Let's say I have some concerns. It's hard for me to believe that anyone would be so careless with so valuable an asset. With that in mind, however, I do not want to lead you in any direction. Best you do that for yourself. I give you free reign to go where you want, when you want. I have no doubt that you could be discreet and keep me informed as frequently as you see fit."

"I appreciate your confidence in my abilities. I hope I can live up to them. I would have to discuss this with my wife, but she has already more or less ordered me to find work. When would you expect me to start and do you have a fee structure in mind?"

"Start tomorrow if you can. As far as fee structure goes, you can have your choice, either an hourly rate or a lump sum arrangement. Frankly I hope you would go for the lump sum because keeping track of hours seems like it would be a pain in the ass."

"What would be the lump sum you clearly have in mind?"

"Of course, I do. I propose a sum of $250,000 to cover your time for up to six months along with an unlimited expense account. The $250,000 would be a retainer and yours to keep regardless how quickly you solve the case. Nothing would please me more than if you came to me after a week with the solution."

"Hah. That would please me as well. Can you get a contact together for me to look at tomorrow?"

"Sure. I just happen to have one here in my briefcase.

Study it overnight and let me know tomorrow."

"You are full of surprises. It's almost like you had this all planned."

"Sure, I did. And for your information I am the majority stockholder in American Independence, so you don't have to worry about the validity of the contract or your ability to enforce it."

"I already knew about your role in Independence, but in any case, I am seeing someone who I would enjoy working with, no matter what your role with the company might be."

"So, I was not the only one doing some checking. I should have known. As far as working with you I have no doubt that you are my type of guy and that we will have a good working relationship, much like you had at Casino Royale, with Roger. I look forward to it. Barring any unforeseen event, I will call you tomorrow morning. I hope to meet you with a signed contract. Take down my private cell number."

I jot down his number and we both leave after he pays the bill. When I call Sam, he lets me know that he is on a lucrative jaunt to Providence. He won't be able to pick me up, so I call an ordinary cab that takes me back to the Inn. When I get there, I find that Gineen has gone out, leaving me a message that she has gone for a walk to our new condo and may look for bicycles at a shop called Landry's on Commonwealth Avenue. It pleases me that she is looking beyond the terror of her cancer – evidence of an inner strength that is way above the ordinary. She arrives back at the inn late in the afternoon, showing no signs of fatigue. Full of sparkles. Once again, before she utters a word, I am reminded how extraordinary this woman is and how much I love her.

"Hi Sherlock. I had a wonderful afternoon. You see my

note?"

"Yes. Tell me about it," I say.

"Well first I walked over to our condo and looked around the place. It is growing on me and I like it more with each visit. The back yard is terrific, and I thought about all the parties we'll have there and how we will outfit it. What I'd like to put there are couple of picnic tables, some comfortable chairs, a gym set for the kids and a wading pool. We will have to add some fencing at the corners of the house with gates on both ends so the kids will be safe."

"Whoa. I love your plan but isn't that getting just a little ahead of ourselves. Last I looked we didn't have any kids. Why don't we wait until we do?"

"No way. When we move in, we'll do all those things. Until we have our own, there are probably kids in the neighborhood who would love to play there. Anybody we entertain would be free to bring along their kids. I don't care if we need to rob a bank to buy it all. It's a done deal."

"OK. But I won't play Clyde to your Bonnie. No need to rob any bank because I have in my hot little hands a contract with the American Independence Insurance Company which comes with a non-refundable retainer of $250,000, subject only to your approval and my signature."

"Lordy, that was fast," she says. "You only just talked to Allen for the first time today."

"My charm oozes from my pores like maple syrup from a tree."

"I think they call that stuff 'sap' which fits much better, in your case."

"He did come to lunch prepared to reel me in," I admit. "Roger may have had something to do with that. We've both had hard days, why don't we eat here at the inn and watch a movie?"

"Oh, I don't think so," she says. "Get on your little computer and find us another grand restaurant where we can celebrate the end of your unemployment properly."

"Nah. Here at the inn is good enough."

"I insist. I'll even pop a bottle of champagne."

"You will? With what?"

"Surprised, are you? You aren't the only one with money. I have a tidy sum of savings that I transferred from the bank in Norwich to a People's United branch in Wellesley. I'm saving that for our first daughter's college education. Besides I have decided that we are not going back to Norwich, so I will sell my condo there. Therefore, I am willing to take a bit of that money to buy you a glass, no I mean a bottle of champagne or even a vineyard."

I ask Google where to go and it tells me the Cask 'n Flagon. Gineen agrees so I dial up Sam and thirty minutes later off we go with Sam driving.

"How did your trip to Providence go, Sam?" I ask.

"Fine. No problem at all. Sometimes I worry about getting stiffed on a long jaunt like that, but I have known this passenger for some time," he explains. "I don't know for sure what he does for a living, only that always tips me big."

Gineen pipes in, "You'd think he would just hop a train at South Station."

"I would, but he likes his privacy. And the door to door service."

"Probably a mafia member. Providence is well known as an active center for their activities."

"Oh Mr. Private Detective you have such a suspicious

mind," Gineen jokes. "Enough of this, here we are at the Flask. Thanks, Sam. Want to join us?"

"Can't do it tonight but maybe another time soon. I can pick you up when you are ready. Give me a call."

"OK. Don't forget that we have a date with you and your wife just as soon as I am out of the woods."

"Right," Sam says and waves us away. "See you later."

CHAPTER III

Cask 'n Flagon is a delightful sports bar with a very unusual menu. It looks like we have made a good choice. After checking the menu, I ask, "What are you going to order, missy?"

"Missy, is it? Well, missy is thinking about chicken tacos and a wedge salad from the lunch menu."

"Sounds like your usual healthy meal. I am doing the 14-ounce New York sirloin with French fries. Hey, do you see any famous athletes here? It is after all a sports bar and we are a stone's throw from Fenway."

"The only athlete I see is sitting across from me," she jokes. "An Olympic eater."

"Have I ever told you that you say the sweetest things?

"I'm sorry. I really don't have any cause for concern. There's not an extra ounce of flab on your lovely body. Forgive me for my nastiness?"

"No apology necessary. I should probably take a lesson from your way of eating anyhow. And, by the way, there's no flab on your body either."

"That's because of all of the horizontal exercising I do. Thanks to my horny honey. Keep up the good work."

The waiter arrives, takes our order and departs for the kitchen. The meal is terrific. I wash it down with a dark beer and decide to follow Gineen's example and omit dessert. I call Sam and he shows up fifteen minutes later.

"Hey, Sam, who's your passenger?" I get into the back seat and gesture to the handsome woman sitting next to him.

"Hey yourself. This the boss of the company who rides with me now and then to make sure that all the proceeds go into the records. Althea, say hello to Patrick Ingel and his wife Gineen."

"Why Gineen, it's nice to meet you. Sam has told me all about you two, but he never told me how beautiful you are."

"Nor did he ever mention that you were beautiful as well," says Gineen.

"Well, Sam, you certainly look handsome," I say jokingly, "but I am sorry to say this detective is no movie star."

"That's true, Sam," Gineen says, "let's drop this goofball off at the inn so the three of us can do the town without his awful sense of humor."

"A nice idea but I am tired after a long day, so I'll just drop the two of you off at the inn and take the boss home."

"Gineen, Sam has told me that you are here for cancer treatment," Althea mentions. "If there is anything I can do to make it easier for you, let me know. Both Sam and I know this city inside and out. My sister had breast cancer and received the best care in the world right here. It wasn't easy, but she survived nicely and has been well since then. Sometimes it's nice to have another woman to talk to and I am a good listener. So, don't be bashful."

"I won't. It's kind of you to offer," Gineen says with a smile.

Sam pulls up to the Inn's front door and we say our goodnights.

We walk through the lobby with me clutching her arm. "They are a dear sweet couple and I hope we see more of them in the future. Preferably outside the confines of that taxicab."

"I have a feeling we will be doing just that. Are you in the mood for a movie tonight?"

"You have something in mind?"

"I do. Juliette Binoche and Clive Owen in *Words and Pictures*. I know we've seen it, but I would like to see it again cuz it's one of my favorite movies."

"Sounds good to me."

We watch this movie and then fall into a sound sleep.

Early in the morning we walk to Dana Farber for Gineen's first appointment. The very first step in the process is the usual hospital check-in routine which consists of the financial details. At the desk, I inform the young woman that I will be paying for the treatment in cash.

"Mr. Ingel, our records show that all of the costs will paid for by a Mr. Roger Jones in Connecticut. Is he a family member?" she asks.

"Not really, just a very close friend."

"You have nice friends. The cost of the treatment is likely to be quite large. We won't know how large until your wife sees the surgeon."

I turn to Gineen and say, "It looks like Roger is always one step ahead of us."

"Y'know, we have talked about this before," Gineen says. "He is doing what he wants to do, so relax."

The woman leads us into an examination room and hands Gineen a hospital gown.

"Take everything off above waist and I will let Dr. Bouno know that you are here. It will be just a few minutes."

Ten minutes later he comes into the room after knocking on the door.

"How do you do, Mrs. Ingel?" he says with an extended hand. "I am David Bouno and I will be in charge of your treatment. How are you today?"

"I'm OK. I guess. Maybe a little scared."

"I've been seeing patients like you for many years and I have to tell you it's normal," he explains. "Everyone gets scared. I already have some background information on you, and I note that you are in excellent physical condition, other than the small cancer in your breast. Let me take a look at the problem. But first do you know if there is any history of breast cancer in your family?"

"If there was, I am totally unaware of it."

He begins to fondle her right breast (well I call it fondling but I don't have a doctor's degree). Gineen and I wince a bit.

"Is there any pain at all?"

"No, none."

"Has there been any pain?"

"No."

"Let's look at your other breast. Good, no sign of any problem there."

"Why don't you get dressed and then come into my office which is just next door?"

Gineen quickly dresses and we sit down with the good doctor in his office.

"Mrs. Ingel, it's never wise to make predictions about cancer, but right now it looks like the problem is relatively small and it was very wise of you to notice it early and come see us so quickly."

"Can you tell me what the treatment will involve?"

"I'd rather not do that until I've had a few days to study the results of today's examination and consult with other members of our team."

"I thought you would be the only one involved with my treatment."

"Not at all," Dr. Buono says. "We work with medical oncologists, surgeons and radiation oncologists. You already know that I will be your surgeon. I will introduce you to the other members before we start any treatment. Are you presently employed? Because, within reason, we'll schedule treatment to fit your situation."

"No, not at all. I am here for treatment and have nothing else to do except move into our new condo. So, three to four days would suit me fine."

"OK. If anything changes, let us know."

"Thanks," Gineen says. Dr. Buono says goodbye to us, and we head to the car.

Walking out to the car, I put my arm around her as if to tell her to hang in there, but she doesn't need it and pushes my arm away. "I'm good and ready for this so don't keep treating me like a baby. The doctor appears to be very conservative and I think we will be fine."

"I promise I won't be a pest, but I just want to make sure that you know that I am here for you no matter what. Nothing in the world is as important as your health and happiness."

"You're sweet and all kidding aside, I love you dearly. Y'think we can move into the condo, say, the day after tomorrow?"

"All we have to do is make sure that we have a bed in there by then. I know how important that it is to you and your exercise routine. Use your charm and get the store to deliver and set it up by the end of the day tomorrow."

"I will do that, so you can continue to perfect your horizontal exercise routine."

"And here I thought it was already perfect."

"Live and learn. It will never be perfect so keep practicing," she says coyly. "Are you ready to start work for the insurance company soon?"

"Yes, if you don't mind," I say. "I think I will head on out to Lincoln and talk to the police this afternoon about the theft."

"Great. Good luck. It feels like a bit of normality is returning to our lives. Get out of here, Patrick."

"OK, boss. Just like old times. You know life is like a ladder and at any time you can choose to step up or step down."

"Some philosopher you are. Now get out quickly before I *fro* you out."

I drive out to Lincoln, which is a toney suburb to the west of Boston, home to some 6,500 people, all of whom appeared to be multi-millionaires many times over by the look of the place. At the police department, I ask to speak to Chief Kennedy, thinking my Irish name might get me started on the right foot. His Irish heritage is reflected in his red hair.

"Good morning, Chief. My name is Patrick Ingel." I shake Chief Kennedy's hand. "I'm a private investigator who has been hired by the American Independence Insurance Company to investigate the details of the Brandt robbery."

"I'm generally familiar with the case since it was so large," he says. "I prefer that you talk to our detective on the case, Doug Milton. Let me get him on the line. I believe he's in the office." He talks to someone briefly on the phone, then hangs up and looks at me. "Ah, he is, so let me show you the way."

He shows me into a small office and introduces me to Milton. His sharp blue eyes survey me quickly as he shakes my hand. He is tall and thin. Impeccably dressed. I wouldn't be surprised if he were an ex-marine. The wealth of the community is reflected in the appearance of the station and most of the personnel in it. There is a feeling of capability that can't be faked.

Milton opens the conversation. "Let me tell you what I know about this case now, and I'll give you the official reports before you leave. First, the Brandt family lives in a very large mansion on Stony Pond Road. The mansion is huge, as are the grounds which are all immaculately manicured. I suspect that in the fall when the leaves are falling off the trees, they never make it to the ground before they are grabbed in the air by the groundskeepers. I don't know how wealthy this family is because it's way above my paygrade to even ask the question. I expect your client would know something about that. Anyhow, the house has about twenty rooms and the grounds encompass about twenty acres. On the night of the theft, all the servants had been given the night off since it was a Saturday night. The only one in the house was the head of the house staff who was asleep on the third floor at the time of the robbery. He would not have been able to hear very much up there. The Brandts, Eloise and Ronald, were at a party at their country club and did not arrive home until two a.m."

I hold up one hand. "Let me interrupt for a minute."

"Sure."

"Did they see any sign of a break-in when they got home?"

I ask.

"They claim they didn't notice any sign when they got home and went straight to sleep. Incidentally, they have a ground floor suite, which a bit unusual for an old mansion like this. The suite was built recently, and I assume that was primarily for the husband who says he has a heart problem. When they awoke next morning, they claimed that the jewelry was gone. That's about it."

"Did they see any signs of a break in?"

"Well there was a broken window in the kitchen but when our technicians were at the scene, it looked like the glass had been broken from the inside. When we confronted them with this, they suggested that perhaps the thief had gotten in via the rear door to the patio. And, for some reason unknown, went out through the kitchen window. Fishy."

"Any signs that the patio door had been jimmied?"

"None that we could see."

"And how did the thief get in the safe?"

"Believe or not," Milton says, "the jewelry was kept in a locked desk drawer in a room they call their office. Every bit of her jewelry that she wasn't wearing that night plus a few very expensive watches of his are gone. The claim totals some ten to fifteen million dollars. Apparently, some of the jewelry is very rare, but you probably know more about that than I do."

"Well I don't yet, but I will. The company must receive a list of the insured items and an appraisal of each one, for the claim to be filed."

"Perhaps you could get us that list as soon as possible so we can canvas the likely places around the region where they might be disposed of."

"I will do that when I get back home later in the day," I agree, jotting something down in a notebook. "I sort of doubt the thief would try to dispose of the items around here. More likely they would do that on the west coast or even in a foreign country. Or perhaps, he or she simply wants to keep it and enjoy looking at it. Thieves are not normal people. But before we go any further, I am going to visit the Brandts in their mansion."

"Good luck to you. Let me know if there is anything else I can do for you. Before you go, I have a packet of all the notes and reports from the Department."

"Thanks," I say and shake Milton's hand one last time. "I'm sure there will things you can help with. Take care."

My Garmin leads me out to the Brandt mansion. The driveway into the house is surrounded by a wall, made of some kind stone that I don't recognize. It is eight feet tall, but the gate is chained in the open position. I guess the wall is a decorative piece and not used for security. I park in front of the door under a very large portico and ring the bell. The door opens immediately, and I am greeted by a person I judge to be the head of the household staff. He has that air about him – a haughty demeanor.

"Good morning sir," he says. "You must be Mr. Ingel. Come right in."

"I am. Patrick Ingel," I say as I extend my hand. "And you are?"

"Sir, I am William Swazey, chief of Mr. Brandt's household staff." He is about six feet tall with thinning gray hair – cut like a marine, perhaps.

"Good morning Bill," I respond in a friendly tone which

seems to piss him off. He grimaces at "Bill." "One of the things I hope to do today is to obtain a list of all the members of your staff including their full names, ages, social security numbers, and the dates they were hired. Please list everyone including the grounds staff. In other words, everyone who works on the premises."

"I'm sorry, Mr. Ingel, but Mr. Brandt would have to OK that list," he says. "Come into his office, he is waiting for you there."

He leads me into a large paneled room which is carpeted in Persian rugs and lighted by Tiffany lamps. A grand chandelier hangs from the middle of the room. Despite the daylight, they are all lit because the windows are hidden by heavy drapes. I am not even sure there are windows behind the drapes. A man, who I assume to be old man Brandt, sits behind a gigantic partner's desk about the size of an aircraft carrier. He looks every bit of his seventy-five years and then some. He is thin and haggard looking.

"Mr. Brandt, this is Patrick Ingel, an investigator working for the insurance company regarding the jewelry theft."

"Good morning, Mr. Brandt. Pleased to meet you." I extend my hand. He looks at it with disdain, ignores it, and says nothing.

This is the way it is, and I have the option of playing along with him or stepping right up and confronting him. Playing his game will get me nowhere so I decide to jump on him right off the bat.

"OK, Brandt let's get one thing straight. I am here on a legitimate mission on behalf of your very own insurance company and your claim for $12,300,000,169.26 dollars will not get paid until I file a report with them. Maybe not even then." I throw in the last bit to stir him up as much as I can.

"You are an impertinent young man. What are you suggesting?" he snarls. "I have been interviewed by police investigators. Whatever you need you may get from them."

"I'm not suggesting anything. I've already interviewed the officer in charge of your theft and his evidence and views will become part of my report. I am conducting an independent investigation for the company, which is their right and duty. If you doubt my word, read your policy. I have already asked your man Swazey for certain information regarding every member of your staff that works here at your home. He all but refused, saying you would have to approve it."

Brandt swings around on his swivel chair. "Just a minute while I talk to my attorney," he says and hunches over the telephone. After a short, whispered conversation, he swivels back to face me. "I wish to cooperate with you to the maximum extent possible as advised by my attorney, Sidney Gerstein."

"Good, then let's get on with my questions."

"Perhaps you should make an appointment with Swazey," Brandt says, gesturing to Swazey. "I must go to my cardiologist in just a few minutes."

"OK and may I have his name?" I am treading water here and under the circumstances have no business with the next inquiry.

Surprisingly, he gives it to me.

"Certainly. Dr. John Swanson. His telephone number is 704-3295. Call him and confirm that I am to see him in just fifteen minutes. I must be going now, so, if you would care to, make an appointment with Mr. Swazey." They both escort me out to the driveway where I get in my car and leave. I call

Swanson on my cell after driving off the estate.

"Good morning, is this Dr. Swanson's office?"

"Yes, it is," a woman's voice says. "This is Nancy, from his nursing staff. How can I help you?"

"This an assistant to Mr. Brandt," I lie. "I am a little bit embarrassed to call you but there was a slight mix-up here this morning. Can you tell me if someone called just a few minutes ago to set an appointment with Dr. Swanson?"

"Why yes, just a few minutes ago. Is there a problem?"

"Oh, no just a personal blunder on my part. I might be in big trouble if Mr. Brandt found out that I called."

"I won't breathe a word."

"Thanks so much. Goodbye."

"Goodbye and have a nice day."

I call Allen's cell and go over the morning's events. "I hope I did right by backing off when I did."

"Oh, you absolutely did. I will, however, call him this afternoon and impress upon him the urgency of seeing you and giving you everything you ask for, as soon as possible. And don't be bashful about questioning him. We have an absolute right to all pertinent information. I am also concerned about the elapsed time from the theft. The jewels could be halfway around the world by now and we will have little chance of finding them."

"Maybe but I have a suspicion in the back of my mind that they are not all that far away."

"Really? And do you have any reason for that suspicion?"

"At this point, only the value of the gems which doesn't seem to justify the trouble and cost of taking them far away and then selling them at a discount from their value, which any thief would have to do. I may be all wet. Only a hunch just now."

"I follow your reasoning and perhaps you are right. We'll see."

"You take care. I am off to meet up with Gineen. Later."

"So long."

I drive back to Brookline and give Gineen a big hug. I see joy in her eyes and it spreads into a smile across her face. "OK, wife. What's up?"

"What's up is that I have managed to arrange for ALL our new furniture to be here by the end of the day tomorrow. We can move in tomorrow night or the day after, for sure."

"I'm so happy and proud to have a wife who exudes charm and uses it so skillfully."

"Well then how about you show your appreciation by taking your charming wife out for a really good lunch," she says. "By tomorrow or the day after you will back to eating tofu for lunch right at home."

"Perish the thought. Let me consult with the Toshiba a minute and we will be off for a splendid lunch." I do some quick research, and immediately come up with somewhere good. "Here we go. It's going to be the Daily Catch for Sicilian seafood right here in Brookline. We don't even need to bother Sam. It's not a long walk down Longwood to Harvard Street, past Coolidge Corner."

"You really don't need to pound all those landmarks into my brain," Gineen says, touching her forehead. "I'll figure them out soon enough."

"I know, love. We are going to live here and be happy, so you need to know these names."

"Sure. I'll try to remember. You ready?"

"Yeah, let's go."

Arm in arm we walk to Coolidge Corner and then to the restaurant. I have a bowl of Sicilian fisherman's stew and a Caesar's salad. I'd rather have a hamburger but it's not on the menu. Don't tell Gineen. She orders clam chowder and shrimp scampi. We chat during lunch about all kinds of things. I bring her up to date on my work for Allen. I find myself staring at her.

"Is my lipstick smeared or what do you see?"

"I see the most beautiful woman in the world, and I think I am falling in love with her again. Will you marry me?"

"As soon as I finish my clam chowder."

We finish lunch and walk leisurely back to the Inn where we have what passes for a nooner.

"OK chief, let's get up and do some vertical exercises."

"Aw, do we have to?"

"Yup. My doctors say I must walk, jog, run, do pushups and all the exercise I want. C'mon. Or do I have to kick your ass out of that bed?"

"Tell you what. You shower, and I will follow. Then you can go downstairs, let them know that we are checking out tomorrow and get a bill. After that, we'll do all the walking and jogging that your little heart desires."

"Little heart? When did I get a little heart?"

"Just a saying, dear heart."

"That's better," she says. "One kiss and I'm off to the shower and the rest of my duties."

It goes according to plan. We walk and jog all the way down and back to the Esplanade and the Hatch Shell. Neither of us pushes very hard but by the time we return, we both are tired in a good kind of way. When we get back, I go up to our room while she goes to the desk to get our bill. I am relaxing when she comes back into the room and says, "You won't like this, but I suggest you don't make a big deal out of it. The bad news is the bill came to just under $2,500. The good news is that it's already been paid by Roger. It makes him feel good, so, please, let it make you feel the same."

"I guess so."

That evening we are too pooped to do anything except watch a movie called *All We Had*, which we both enjoyed. After the movie we fall sound asleep. Bright and early the next morning we say our goodbyes to the Inn and walk down to our new home. It's early enough that no deliveries have been made and the place is empty. We sit on the floor in a corner holding hands. After a while Gineen turns to me with a few tears in her eyes.

"We are truly home, aren't we? Oh, I am happy and sad at the same time. I suppose that breaking with the past is always sad. We had a good time at the Casino, didn't we?"

"Indeed, we did. Mostly good times and they will live with us for a long time. But I prefer to think about the future. It will be even better. I know it. You will make a great mother and I will learn how to be a good father and not make the same mistakes that I did in the past. I can see Mark and Cynthia visiting and even having a good time with our kids."

Mark and Cynthia are my two kids from my first failed marriage. Much of the blame for that failure is on my shoulders, but not all of it. Anyhow, that is ancient history.

"Hey, slow down. You are wearing me out already. But I really do like your picture. We will make it happen, won't we?"

"You bet."

It's ten and the first of our furniture arrives. "A bed. A good sign, woman. Let's try it out as soon as they leave.

"Remember all those nice things I just said. Forget them, pig."

"But I'm your pig."

Little by little the furniture arrives and is set up. I spend the entire day there with Gineen and by the end of the afternoon her spirits are on high. "I'm glad you didn't run off and leave me to manage the furniture setup by myself. You are part of this home and it would only be a condo without you. To show you how much that means to me I am going to treat you to a grand dinner right here in our new home. You'll have to forgive me for all this gushing, but I have such warm feelings. You go out into the back yard and put together an inventory of things we will need to make it a safe and fun place for us and the kids."

"Hey, now who's rushing things? There are no kids yet."

"Sure, there are. I've seen them running around the neighborhood. Be sure to include a small jungle gym and pool."

"So, is it your intention to make this a neighborhood park?"

"Sometimes you are slow for a really bright guy. The kids have parents, who I hope will become friends and these small play things will encourage them to come over with their kids. Hop to it!"

"Yes, boss." Following orders, I retire to the back yard and make my list which includes some fencing to make it fully enclosed as well as the jungle gym, the pool, a picnic table, a lawn mower to cut the grass and a garden hose to fill the pool and water the grass. A sprinkler and who knows what else. Oh hell, I'll need a storage shed for all the things on the list. The picture developing in my mind is not a pretty one for me. It's been some time since I was a domesticated husband and it'll take some time to get comfortable. By that time, I will have finished with the measurements, it is dinner time at the Ingel home. I keep rolling the words Ingel home around in my mind and I decide I like them. Maybe this time I will be a real husband and father.

"Oh my, something smells delicious. Goodness, candlelight and is that a bottle of champagne in that bucket? Somebody has been doing some planning for this grand event and there's only one other person here."

"Well, I feel like I am raising the curtain on a grand event with a grand husband and it should be marked by a grand feast for us. There is a filet mignon for you and scallops for me and yes that is a bottle of champagne. I believe it's the head of the house who generally does the toast. So, here's to a long and fruitful married life!"

"Hey, I thought it was generally the man who is considered the head of the house."

"True, but it's good to break with tradition sometimes. And this is one of those times. Drink up!"

"Well, I am in charge of the back yard and any toasting done out there will be by me," say I, trying save a little face.

"Absolutely, master of the back yard. I will drink to that. OK, no more toasting until I can fetch dinner from the kitchen. Keep your hands away from that bottle."

She returns with a rare filet for me with a baked potato with sour cream and chives and corn on the cob dripping with butter. A salad and sautéed bay scallops for her.

"I will gladly relinquish my God-given role as household

head if this is a sample of the menu that results."

"Umm. occasionally, it's OK but we have to get you on a healthy diet soon. Then you can produce healthy kids."

"I'll remind you that I have already produced healthy kids without the help of fish."

The meal is nothing short of the best of Manhattan. We polish off the champagne without any trouble.

"You do the dishes and clean up the kitchen and I will go upstairs and select a movie."

I do the assigned chores without bitching because that is our deal, one cooks, the other one cleans up.

Upstairs we watch *Million Dollar Baby* where Hilary Swank manages to land a lot of punches and Clint Eastwood just manages.

"I hope you don't get any wild ideas from this," I say to Gineen.

For that I get a blow to the solar plexus. I almost lose my filet. I forget what a sweet and caring soul she is and how she seems to love beating up on me. Some things never change.

"The only way I know to stop you from beating me up is to make mad passionate love to you."

I slowly remove all our clothes and proceed to do the mad passionate thing.

"Umm. Don't go away I believe I need a curtain call or two. Lights, cameras, action."

I comply. After all, an order is an order, even in the theater. After episode two, we fall into a sound sleep and I don't wake up until a few hours later when she starts nibbling around my belly button.

"Stop it woman, you will kill me."

"Do you know a better way to die?"

"Stop, stop. I quit. I give up. That's all for tonight or I'll tie you down to the bed, I will."

"Ooh, that's an idea we haven't tried yet. Alright, I think I get the message. One more kiss and then, goodnight."

We hug and kiss tenderly one more time and then it's off to a sound sleep in 8.5 seconds for this 39-year-old body. Maybe we have discovered a new sleep remedy. Trouble is I can't patent it and anyway most everyone in the world already knows about it.

CHAPTER IV

Next morning at breakfast, I tell Gineen I am going to leave her for a few hours to talk once more with Allen's recalcitrant customer.

"I'm guessing that it will take me about three hours to do it, so I may be back by lunch but don't get worried if it takes a bit longer. Brandt has not been very forthcoming thus far and I don't suppose he's had a great epiphany since I saw him last."

"Sounds like he has something to hide."

"Doesn't it?"

"If you leave me your list of things for the back yard, I will see what I might be able to locate for you while you are gone. I'll wait for lunch until you get back. No champagne though."

"Great. See you then."

On the way out to Lincoln, I call Allen and he tells me that he has contacted Brandt and told him to expect me. He also told him in no uncertain terms that his claim will not be paid until he has cooperated with me and my investigation has been completed. We'll see. I'm not expecting much.

When I ring the bell, I am greeted cordially by Swazey, Brandt's chief honcho, "Good morning, Mr. Ingel. Mr. Brandt is waiting for you in the breakfast room."

Indeed, Brandt is seated at a large table, surrounded

by an enormous array of every conceivable breakfast food imaginable. A few that I can't imagine or identify.

"Good morning, Mr. Ingel. Have you had breakfast? Swazey, fetch Mr. Ingel a plate."

"No sir. I've had breakfast, but coffee would be fine." And indeed, the coffee, poured from a silver pot, is as fine as I have ever tasted.

"How are you, Mr. Ingel? I had a call from Mr. Allen, advising that you would be here today. I will happily supply whatever information you need. In fact, I have already obtained a copy of the police report which should tell you everything I know about the theft."

"Mr. Brandt, we seem to be stuck in a rut. You know as well as I do that I already have the police reports and have spoken at length with the chief," I say, sipping my coffee. "Let me renew my prior request. I need a complete list of the names and addresses of all the employees who work here on your estate. I need any knowledge you may have relative to their criminal history, if any. I need the names of all your business enterprises, either here in the U.S. or abroad, along with the names of the directors of each company. A copy of the last annual report for each one completes the list."

"Mr. Ingel, what possible connection could my companies have with the theft?" he asks, his voice genuine. "You are reaching quite far."

"Perhaps so, and if my investigation concurs that there is no connection, I will say that. Until then, everyone in the world is a possible suspect. That's routine for an investigation of this large a claim. I know that Mr. Allen would concur. Call him and check it out if you like. If he tells me I am out of bounds with any of these items, so be it."

"It won't be necessary to call him. I will get you everything you asked for, but please be discreet with all these individuals. Let me call Swazey and get the list of employees. Start with that and we will go from there."

He summons Swazey and tells him to get me the list of employees. Swazey complies.

"Sir, if you could come back tomorrow morning, I will have the list for you," he says with a nod.

"Is there some kind of problem with getting it now? I will certainly wait here while you put it together. I won't be able to come back tomorrow because my wife is starting cancer treatment in the morning."

Swazey looks at his boss for a split second, who gives him a barely perceptible positive shake of the head.

"I hope everything works out well for your wife." The words come out of his mouth in a disingenuous tone as if he is reading me the weather report.

"Come with me to the office and I will get the list."

I follow him to his office, expecting to wait while he compiles a list from payroll records or some other source. Instead he hands me a list already made up. While I am looking it over, I ask, "Is this a current list as of this week?"

"Yes, it is."

"Have you fired anyone recently or has anyone quit?"

"No sir," he replies. "Neither."

"Are you aware that any of them have criminal records? Been charged with a crime or convicted?"

"None."

"Not even unpaid parking tickets?"

"Sir, we don't go into that kind of detail."

"When you said that none of them have criminal records,

what was that based on? Any searching of the police or court records?"

"No sir. It's based on the employees' sworn statements."

I guess he believes a criminal would not possibly lie about a record. I let it go. I will follow up on my own. Easy enough to do.

"Thank you, Swazey. Before I leave, please remind Mr. Brandt of the rest of the data that I requested. I will be back to him within a few days."

"You're welcome and I surely will remind him. Good day sir."

What a cold fish. Even colder than his boss, who at least tries to sound genuine, even if he's not. Although I have gathered some data from this trip, I come away with a serious lack of trust in either one of them.

Probably my dreaming but on the way back to the condo I swear I am being tailed by someone in a late model red Cadillac. If I am being followed that guy couldn't have chosen a more conspicuous car. I stick this into a corner of my brain. When I get back to our condo, I tell Gineen about what I have learned, she lifts an eyelid and says, "It sounds like you have your work cut out for you. Are you going back there tomorrow?"

"You can't be serious," I say incredulously. "Your treatment starts tomorrow. I will be with you as long as it takes for you to be comfortable."

"I am determined to face this and beat it. It isn't necessary for you to hold my hand all the way."

"It may not be necessary but that's the way it will be. No discussion allowed. One word and I will pull a Gineen and whack you in the stomach."

She puts her arms around me and says to me in a shaky voice, "I promised myself I would not be a burden to you and I meant it. At the same time, I know deep down I can't make it without some help from you. Now, let me get lunch together."

"Sure, but tonight we are going out for dinner and dancing."

"Thank you, dear heart. You are the best."

"Nah, I'm next to the best right this moment and I plan to be there forever."

We spend the afternoon putting the finishing touches on our new home. We play all kinds of pop music and mostly putter around the place. While she is fussing around in the kitchen, the phone rings and it's Roger.

"Hello Patrick. It came to me this morning that Gineen starts her treatment tomorrow. I wish I could be there, but I just can't. When I finish talking to you, I want to speak to her. In the meantime, I wanted to let you know that I have arranged for 24-hour home care for her. I have hired two nurses to stay at my condo. I will give you their names before I have finished talking to Gineen. She is so independent that she probably will not react well to this, but between the two of us, we will convince her that a little help is OK."

"Roger, that's more than I would ever ask of you but by now I know what a tyrant you are, so I won't argue. Let me get Gineen."

I find Gineen in the kitchen and give her the phone and leave the room, so they can talk in private.

Ten minutes later I hear her call me in with a weepy voice. "Did he tell you what he wants to do? Supply me with two nurses to help take care of me during the treatment."

"We did talk about it and don't even think about giving him a hard time about it. It would break his heart."

"I won't. I won't. He is such a dear man, like a father to me." At that she comes into my arms and sobs violently for a few minutes.

"Hey, you are getting my shirt all wet. Knock it off."

That does it. She steps back, hauls off and slams in the stomach, her favorite target.

"Hey, you didn't have much *oomph* behind that one." I break away before she can try again.

"Patrick. Thanks for the invitation for a date out on the town today but would you mind if we just stayed in tonight? We could light up the fireplace and order some Asian take-out. That would satisfy my mood just now."

"I'm good with that. Why don't you get into your pajamas while I call the restaurant, and then get a fire started?"

"You mean you don't want me to put on a sexy negligee?"

"I'll leave that up to you, but it is a bit chilly in here."

I light the fire and call for the food and shortly she comes back, not only in her pjs but also with big furry slippers on her feet.

"Too chilly in here for a negligee."

When the food arrives, we sit down on our sofa facing the fireplace and enjoy the food.

The meal finished, I suggest that we open the sleep sofa and spend the night right there in front of the fireplace.

"I accept the invitation. I am just a little nervous about tomorrow and might keep you awake, so you can sleep by yourself upstairs, if you want."

"No way, but try not to knock me off the bed."

"l won't. A bed without you is no bed at all."

"You say the sweetest things. But then again if performance in bed were an Olympic sport, you would likely be a world champion."

"Well, of Boston, at least. Good night hon."

"Good night to you."

CHAPTER V

At breakfast the next morning I inform Gineen that I intend to call Sam and ask him to pick us up and wait until we are done.

"That's a waste of money," she says, a shake in her voice. "Let's just walk over there and we'll see how I feel when it's over."

"Nope. I insist."

When I call Sam and ask if he can pick us up and stay with us at Dana Farber, he answers, "I would feel bad if you hadn't asked. What time should I show up?"

"Today's appointment is at ten so pick us up at quarter of?"

When we arrive, we note that the surgery is done at a section of the hospital called the Susan B. Smith Center and we are checked in there, quickly and easily since the paperwork has already been done. We accompany a nurse into Dr. Lindlys' office where introductions follow.

"Good morning, I am Charles Lindlys." He reaches out to shake her hand.

"Good morning, I am Gineen Ingel." Gineen shakes his hand. "Nice to meet you."

"Likewise, although I wish it could be under happier circumstances. This must be your husband, Patrick.

"Yes, nice to meet you."

"OK, let's get right to it. Our past examination leads us to believe that because you caught this at a very early stage, the likelihood is that you will not require radical surgery. We see no signs that the cancer has spread to any other organ in your body. Having said that, there are no guarantees with this disease, and it is my intention to use all our available techniques to give you the best chance at a complete cancer free recovery."

"Does that mean chemotherapy?"

"It does. In your case it seems wise to me to also use radiation to further ensure that we rid the body of any traces."

"Does that mean I will lose my hair?"

"That's possible but we can't predict that with certainty. I won't lie to you. You are likely, no, let's say certainly, to be a sick young woman for a while, so you shouldn't schedule any important work for the next few weeks until your body tells you that it's OK. On the other hand, it's helpful to be as active as you can."

I am listening silently to this doctor-patient dialogue when I feel some bad vibes from Gineen. I make a feeble try to inject some levity into this gloomy conversation, "Good, this means she can cook, do the dishes, and clean the condo."

"Funny, Patrick!!" she says with a soft slap to my shoulder. "Doctor, perhaps we can get a brain transplant for him while we're here. Otherwise, just ignore him. Patrick, out to the waiting room so the good doctor can get started."

I give her a hug and a kiss and head for the waiting room where I wait, not knowing what to expect. Sam and I wait for an eternity, until Gineen finally comes into the room escorted by a nurse. I am uncertain whether to hug her. She says, "It's OK, detective. I won't break."

I hug and kiss her and ask uncertainly, "Can we go home, or do you have to hang around here for a while?"

"We're free to go but I can't operate heavy machinery for the rest of the day."

"That's too bad; I haven't finished fencing in the back yard. I will hold off on it until tomorrow morning, so you can do it then."

"Hilarious. Here take my free chemo capsules. Don't lose them. Hi Sam, thanks so much for waiting for us. You are an angel."

"Not yet but when you have been cancer free for a year, I will turn into one just for you. Right now, I am just a cab driver."

After Sam drops us off at the condo, I put my arm around Gineen and help her into the condo.

"I think I will take a little nap. I feel a little weary, but I'm glad the hard part is over."

"Let me make you some chicken soup with matzoh balls. My Jewish friends tell me it cures anything."

"Oh. I didn't know you had any Jewish friends."

"A bit of an exaggeration. I read it in a book somewhere. I think it was in the waiting room a few minutes ago."

"Y'know, it doesn't sound like a bad idea. Whip some up and I'll see how I feel about it when I get up."

"Want some matzoh balls with it?"

As I take her arm and help her up the stairs, I whisper in her ear, "If I knew that chicken gumbo would make you feel better, I would find out how to make it and whip up a couple of gallons of it."

"You are a sweet man and I love you dearly, but plain chicken soup will be fine. See you in a while."

It breaks my heart to see her hurting, but I remind myself that I won't do her any good being a wimp. Downstairs I am looking for a can of chicken soup when the telephone rings and it's Roger.

"Good morning, Patrick. It's Roger. How did the treatment go?"

"Good morning, yourself. The doctor is great and at this point he feels the results are as good as can be expected. He tends to keep us grounded and is conservative when he talks about the future."

"Sounds good. May I speak to Gineen?"

"She's upstairs napping. I'm sure she'll want to talk to you. Will you be at the Casino this afternoon?"

"I will. I talked to the two nurses today. They will be moving into my condo this afternoon. Their names are Cynthia Gardener and Frances Gensberg. They will knock on your door when they arrive."

"Roger, I know that Gineen will give you a hard time about needing that help but don't let her talk you out of it. I think it's a good idea."

"Don't worry, I won't."

"Will we see you soon? I believe that would be great medicine for her."

"Yes. Sometime this week, for sure. Got to run."

"Take care."

I spend the rest of the morning making a check list for Gineen's chemo pills first and then thinking about my problem with the jewelry theft. I pull out the list of employees at the mansion. First on the list is Swazey, the underboss. There is a cook, a butler, three cleaning personnel, two drivers, six groundskeepers, and one security guard. The last person on the list is named Elvin Ponce. Interesting. He is listed as a security guard. I wonder where Mr. Ponce was at the time of the robbery. I plan to interview him first, but before I do, I plan to run a records' check on him to see if his sworn statement on his employment application is correct. Start with that. I do that right away. I call Sally Langone at the Connecticut DMV, a person who has helped me many times in the past.

"Sally Langone," she says when she answers. "How may I help you?"

"Sally, Patrick Ingel. How are you?" I say. "I wondered if you were still there."

"I am, but not for long. I'm going on an extended leave in a couple of weeks. How are you and Gineen?"

"She started her chemotherapy and radiation today so right now she is upstairs resting."

"Roger told me that was about to happen. Please give her my very best. Roger and I hope to see the two of you soon."

Aha. I knew there was a developing romance between the two of them. I couldn't be more pleased. It will be good for them.

"One more favor if you can, Sally. Can you give me the name of a person in the Mass. Registry of Motor Vehicles who I might trust to make some discreet inquiries?"

"Try Inspector Marshal Simpson. He's a good guy and will be discreet."

"Thanks, Sally. See you soon." I hang up after she gives me his number. I plan to call him later but right now, I want to see how Gineen's doing, so I tip toe up the stairs. The door is closed but inside the bathroom I can hear gagging sounds and I know she is throwing up. I wait until I hear the bathroom door opens into the suite.

"Having a rough time, I see."

"You better believe it. My entire digestive system is completely empty, and I feel weak as a pussy cat."

"It's time for something to eat, how about some chicken broth?" I hear the doorbell ring downstairs. "Oh, hell. Who can that be at the door? Hang on, I'll be right back."

Two lovely women are at the door who introduce themselves as Cynthia Gardiner and Frances Gensberg, the two nurses hired by Roger.

"Your timing is impeccable. Gineen is upstairs and she has been vomiting her guts out. And if I know her, she is getting ready to come down here and go to work in the kitchen."

They follow me up the stairs and sure enough Gineen, pale as ghost, is changing into blue jeans and about to head downstairs.

"Gineen, this is Cynthia Gardiner and Frances Gensberg, the two nurses that Roger hired to help you in your recovery."

"Honestly, I'll be fine in a few minutes."

"Sure, after you've fallen down the stairs and broken your neck. Now please stay here and rest some more. Follow their instructions. They know what they are doing."

Gardiner is the younger of the two and Gensberg seems to be in charge. She moves right in and puts her arm around Gineen's shoulder and leads her to the bed. "Your body is talking to you," she says calmly. "You've just had a difficult treatment and you need rest. Between the three of us we can help soften your recovery. Don't fight the need to sleep. You should be eating lightly and frequently to deal with the nausea. We have a proscribed diet and will be here to prepare it. Your only job is to get stronger. OK?"

"Well, OK. I do feel a little weak," Gineen agrees as she climbs into bed. She is soundly asleep in minutes.

"I really appreciate having you two around. Gineen is a tough cookie and would probably be out cutting the grass if we let her."

Fran nods knowingly. "We pretty much got the lowdown from Mr. Jones when he hired us, so you can relax. Cynthia, you watch the patient while Patrick shows me around the place and the condo next store where we will be staying for the time being."

"Does this mean that you will be watching her twenty-four hours a day?"

"No. I don't think that is necessary at all. One of us will be here twenty-four hours day and certainly on call at any time. Mr. Jones explained that you are a private investigator and are working on a difficult case. So, go and do, freely. If it involves night work, let us know and we'll be here if you think we are needed."

"Let me thank you up front. I like the way you gained her confidence so quickly. She seems to trust you already."

"Thanks. When you have been doing nursing as long as I have, you learn a few things about people over and above the medical aspects."

By this time, I have shown her around the place and given her keys to both places.

"You go ahead and go to work. Thanks for the keys. Cynthia will stay and watch, and I will go out and shop for some food for her and stock up the condo next door."

"I'm delighted that you are here. I'll be out for a few hours. See you in the middle of the afternoon."

CHAPTER VI

My first stop is the Massachusetts Registry of Motor Vehicles where I ask to see Inspector James Marshall, as suggested by Sally Langone. He is on the phone when I get there but ten minutes later, he comes out and introduces himself, "Good Morning, I'm Inspector Marshall. What can I do for you?"

"Hi. I'm Patrick Ingel," I say, shaking his hand firmly, "a private investigator."

"Aha. Sally Langone told me you were coming over. Come on into my office where we can talk."

He takes a seat behind a desk and motions me to a chair.

"Sally tells me you are working on a large theft case. How can I help?"

Direct and to the point. I like his style immediately. "I'm looking for any background information on an individual and thought you might be able to help."

"Name?"

"Elvin Ponce. When did he get his license? Where did he come from prior to his present residence? Instate or out of state? Criminal record, if any, and any other information you might have available, so I can build a complete profile on him. I know this would require some considerable work on your part and am I'm willing to pay a reasonable fee for it."

"Tell you what. Let me gather together the data I can find, and I'll call you. We can meet somewhere for a beer. I have twenty-five years in here, with a good pension available and I am frankly getting tired of all the bureaucratic goings on. I'd like to pick your brain about private detective work. Deal?"

"Deal. I'll go for two beers. Give me a call when you're ready. Any idea how long?"

"Probably by tomorrow."

"Great." I reach into my pocket and pull out a handful of cards. I hand him one and say, "Here's my card."

After I've left his office, I realize I may be able to use him to gather similar data on the entire staff at the mansion. I stick that idea in the corner of my brain. Do brains really have corners? That covers Brandt's known employees at the mansion. Getting any information on his business enterprises is clearly going to be more difficult and I need to noodle about this for a while. I wonder if I should get some advice from Allen, so I pull out my cell and call him.

"Allen. Good morning. How are you? Listen, can you break away for lunch at Jake Worth's?"

"For you, of course. Besides it's been a boring day around here. Twelve thirty, OK?"

"See you there." I get there before he does, get a table and order a beer. He arrives fifteen minutes later when I have just ordered my second beer. "Hi, Harry. Have a seat. I'm one beer ahead of you."

"What gives with this Harry shit? I told you I don't recognize that name. Allen is fine. Nobody calls me Harry or Harold because I hate the name."

"How about at home. Certainly, your wife doesn't call you Allen, does she?"

"Never mind. None of your business."

He seems genuinely pissed off, so I drop this line of

questioning.

"I thought it would be a good time to give you a progress report. I need some advice, as well."

"Why don't we order first? I'm going to have Weiner Schnitzel."

"And I'll have Jaeger Schnitzel and an order of Jaeger Frites. Gineen probably wouldn't approve. Just in case you bump into her, keep it to yourself."

"Sure."

"I had a meeting with an investigator at the Registry of Motor Vehicles named Marshall. He is building a file on Brandt's security guard, one Elvin Ponce. I thought I'd start with him since security was his responsibility. An obvious place to begin. I will do the same for all the employees, but I don't want to wear out my welcome with Marshall since I feel that he may be an asset in the future. So, from here on I intend to pay him for any additional files. You don't have a problem with that, do you?"

"Not with paying him but I wonder about the wisdom of bringing him into the investigation at all. Remember, we talked about too many cooks spoiling the broth. With the names you are giving him, he certainly will have no trouble figuring out what you are working on."

"I know, but I had no choice except to get someone to find the data for me. You're right, he probably has already figured out what I am working on, but I feel confident he will be discreet with that information. I am meeting him for lunch tomorrow to pick up the data on Ponce. He mentioned that he is considering retiring from the state and going into private practice. He wants to pick my brains about that at lunch. He offered to trade the file for a chance to do that over a beer or two. I'm just about certain that if he does decide to retire, he will be an asset to us."

"OK. You have convinced me. You go ahead with him. What else?"

"I asked Brandt for information about his business enterprises and I sense he is not about to give me anything having to with his business side."

"Probably not. We are skirting the edge on that issue. I doubt that we are legally entitled to it."

"Anything you know might be helpful."

"Well, about all I know is name of his umbrella corporation. It's simply named Brandt Importing, but you could have gotten that from Google."

"I suppose, but I haven't quite given up the notion that he will give us some details about it."

"Give it up. He won't be volunteering it. On the other hand, if you were to discreetly make some forays under that rock, you never know what you might find. Just keep me and my board of directors out of it."

"Will do. Count on it. Thanks for lunch, Allen."

"No problem and give my good wishes to your wife, Ingel."

CHAPTER VII

At home, Fran is there and Gineen is asleep upstairs. "How has she been?" I ask.

"Normal for a patient who just had radiation and chemotherapy," Fran explains. "In other words, sick as a dog."

"Did she have lunch at all?"

"She did. A bit of chicken soup and half a slice of toast. It stayed down which is a good sign. In lots of similar cases the patients go for days without being able to keep food down."

"Great, I'm so glad you're here. I'm going out on some errands. Is there anything I can get you?"

"As a matter of fact, yes there is," she says. "Could you pick me up some regular tea, not decaffeinated like you have in the pantry? Oh, and some dark chocolate."

"Sure. Just don't let Gineen see it. Candy is on her no-no list so when I want some, I have to sneak it into the house and into my mouth."

"As a trained nurse, I see no evil, hear no evil."

"I like that attitude."

My real purpose for the trip is to buy a bunch of flowers and plants to brighten up the condo. I do that. I also get a piece of foam core and some magic markers to make some signs and of course, some chocolate for Fran (and some for me; man is not made of stone).

When I return to the condo, Gineen is still sleeping and

Fran is in the living room reading a mystery story, *the Million Dollar Typewriter* by Murray Segal. I spread the potted plants and flower bouquets around the lower floor. The sign I make reads, *To the Sweetest Woman A Man Ever Had*. I plant it over the fireplace where she will see it when she comes down the stairs.

"Speaking of sweet, Gineen is lucky to have such a sweet husband."

"When you get to know her better, you will realize that I am the lucky one. I'm going out to work on the back yard."

First things first. I dig four holes for the section of fencing that will close in the back yard and fix them in with stones and mortar which I mix up myself. While they are setting, I manage a bit of landscaping and plant some shrubs to cover portions of the fence. I bolt the picnic table together and inflate the small kid's pool. All this takes me a couple of hours and suddenly the rear door opens and Gineen steps out.

"You are such a sweet man. Inside and outside, everything you have done is more than beautiful."

I walk over to the door, hug her gently and whisper in her ear, "All I want is for you to be healthy and happy."

"Look what you've done. The picnic table, the kid's pool and everything. I can't wait to meet some of the neighbors and have them over."

"When your body is ready for that, it will tell you."

"Not strong enough for anything like that yet. Patrick, look at me. Do you see anything different about me?"

Besides being pale and tired looking, no I don't. What are you worried about?

"Oh, God. I'm losing my hair," she sobs.

"What are you talking about. You haven't lost any hair."

"You can't see it because it's just started. But I just brushed my hair and the brush was full of hair," she sobs.

"Calm down, Gineen. If you really are losing hair, which I doubt, it will grow back as beautiful as ever." Her long black hair draped over her oval shaped face is the highlight of her physical beauty, and I understand her angst.

"You're right. I get so emotional over little things now. I feel so ashamed of myself after you have done all this lovely work. Please forgive me."

"Gineen. There is nothing to forgive you for. This is hard stuff you are going through. I know I couldn't handle it as well as you are. Let me get some chairs and we'll sit out here and soak up some rays."

"Sure. You are the absolute sweetest man alive. I feel better already."

I get chairs and we spend hours in the sun, reading and chatting about everything and nothing, lost in each other.

It's five o' clock when Cynthia comes out and tells Gineen that it's time for something to eat.

"I'm going to make you some broth. Shall I bring it out here? It's very lovely here. Sunny and peaceful."

"Thanks to the handiwork of the best and most talented husband in the world."

"That's quite an endorsement," Cynthia said.

"That's because she's stuck with me for life and knows it," I say. "No way she gets rid of me, ever."

"Sure, bring the broth out here and we'll have a picnic," Gineen agrees.

"Here we are, having our first picnic in the back yard. The

first of many. The kids are going to have a ball here," I say nodding to the back yard as Gineen drinks her broth. "Gineen, tomorrow I'm going to do some more work. I have a lunch scheduled with an inspector from the DMV that may take some time."

"If you are apologizing again for working, please stop it or I'll show you just how well I'm coming back with a left to the jaw."

"Ah, floats like a butterfly, stings like a bee."

"You makin' fun of me?"

"Nah. Too scared. I need love, not punches."

"You can have both, silly man. Is the inspector at the Registry Sally Langone's counterpart in Massachusetts?"

"She actually gave me his name and has worked with him before. But he is older and has more depth of investigative experience. He said he is thinking of retiring from the state and wants to pick my brains about work in the private sector."

"A more verdant field to pick in, I can't imagine."

"Now you are the one making fun. It shows me that you are already are getting stronger. Anyhow, I think he might be helpful in my case."

"Is Allen OK with that?"

"We have an agreement to keep the number of people working on the investigation to a minimum, so I will have to make sure that he will be an asset before I take it to Allen."

"Sounds to me like you are going to need some help on this one. Brandt and crew aren't cooperating and aren't like to be any easier to pry information out of in the future."

"You've got that right. It is nice out here if I don't say so myself."

"Sorry I said anything. Seriously, I feel so much better out here, both physically and mentally. I keep having images in the future with children playing here. It doesn't scare me at all. I look forward to it happily."

"I do too. You are starting to look a bit tired. Want to go inside and rest?"

"You mean rest so I can go to sleep? I guess I should. Will you stay with me and hold me?"

"I look forward to it. Let me help you," I say as I try to help her up the one step into the house.

"Cut it out, Patrick. Damn. You can hold me but don't baby me ever."

"Sorry. I just want to make it as easy as possible. I promise I'll stop."

In the house, I tell Cynthia that we are in for the night and she should take off.

"Sure. You guys take care and have a good evening. Don't forget both of us are just next door. If you need us, just call."

"Thanks, Cynthia. I will. And you have a good evening too."

I open the sleep sofa to do some reading. After an hour, I ask, "Want to watch a movie?"

"How about just some music? Start with Dusty Springfield and go from there."

I turn on the music and before the end of the Springfield album, she is sound asleep in my arms. I turn off the lights and hold her the rest of the night. She sleeps all through the night. I take that to be an excellent sign.

Fran is back just before breakfast. She expresses some surprise as Gineen comes down the stairs.

"Well, don't you look good? How is the nausea this morning?"

"Better, thank you. I think I'd like to try some scrambled eggs for breakfast. You think that would be alright?"

"Well, honey it seems a bit heavy, but we have to go by what your stomach is telling you. Why don't we start with just one egg and see how that goes?"

"Sure. Patrick, do you have to sit there gobbling down home fries and bacon? Perhaps you could eat in the office," she snaps. "I'm sorry, it's just hard for me."

"Oh, nothing to apologize for. I understand. If I were in your place, I would probably go mad. I am going to the office to eat and then do some work."

In the office, I open a notebook and make a list of the employees at the mansion and what little I know about each one, which is not much. I call Marshall and ask him to meet me at P.F. Chang, a Chinese Restaurant in the Cambridgeside Galleria which is in Cambridge but not very far from his office in Boston. "Why don't we meet at 11:30?"

"See you then." I figure the restaurant is far enough out of the way so there would be little likelihood of him bumping into any of his co-workers.

The crew cut, burly figure of Marshall marches into the restaurant exactly at 11:30. Every aspect of his demeanor has a military feel to it. I shake his outstretched hand and pay the price for that.

"Good morning, Inspector Marshall."

"If we are going to work together, you'd better drop that Inspector Marshall crap. Everyone around my shop just calls me Jim. OK?"

"Sure, and I'm Patrick. Nobody ever calls me Pat or Paddy or anything else, on the penalty of death."

We get a table and order lunch. When the waiter has left, Jim reaches into his briefcase and takes out a few pages, which he immediately starts to condense for me. Sort of like a military debriefing. I wonder if I should stand and salute. He has done a remarkable job on researching the background on one Mr. Elvin Ponce. All thoughts about his military bearing leave my head as he summarizes.

"Your Mr. Ponce currently lives in Worcester; in what you and I would call a working class, blue collar neighborhood. There is a photo of his house as well as a copy of his driver's license in this file. He has lived there for about two years. He has a mortgage on the place for about 40% of its value and comes up with the payment like clockwork, never having missed a payment in the two years. I have not tried to get into his bank account, but I probably could if you need that information."

"Excuse me for interrupting but for the time being hold off on that. What bank does he use?"

"Well, all I know so far is that his mortgage payments are drawn on a branch of TD Bank. He may have accounts at other banks."

"Good, thanks."

"Prior to the present, his last place of residence was Elks Grove Village, Illinois. This is a small-town close to O'Hare Airport in Illinois. The records show that he was employed at the airport as a security guard. Essentially the same sort of job he has at Brandt's Mansion."

"Does the report say why he left O'Hare?" I ask.

"No. I haven't gotten that far," Marshall admits. "I suppose I could check with the Airport's personnel office. They might talk to me if I approached them with a good story."

"Why not tell them you are checking on him on behalf of a new employer? That's a bit of a stretch but who cares?"

He shrugs. "I don't, if you don't."

"OK then. Go ahead with an approach. Let me know what you find out as soon as you can. Anything else in your report?"

"No, sir. That about wraps it up for today."

I pay the bill and head back to the condo where I find that Gineen has had a small relapse with the nausea after lunch. Fran is there when I open the door.

"Patrick, she's upstairs and sleeping," Fran says. "Did some vomiting again after lunch, so we gave her something for it and put her to bed." She reads the look on my face and quickly continues, "Don't be alarmed this is not unusual and she is fine, just very tired."

"If it's OK with you, I'll just go quietly peek at her."

"Sure."

Internally, my heart is breaking, and I feel so frustrated that I can't make this business go away. I tiptoe up the stairs and quietly crack the door to look at her.

"What do you think I am, an art exhibit?" she jokes from bed. "Come on in, bozo. I won't break."

My heart is about to break in two as I bend over the bed, cup her face in my hands and kiss her forehead. She is pale and sleepy looking, but a small grin forms at the corner of her mouth. "Gotcha. Now get the hell out of my bedroom so I can sleep. You get no sex tonight."

By the time I back out of the door there are light snoring noises coming from her mouth and I relax a little. Downstairs, I look at Fran let her know that her patient is resting. "I think she'll be out for hours, maybe all night. Thanks for helping her and letting me peek."

"Just doing my job."

"And doing it so well," I say. "Gineen really has such confidence in you and so do I."

I give her a quick hug and go into the office to do some more scheming. I barely start to scribble some notes when the phone rings and it is Marshall.

"Hey, that was fast work," I say, balancing the phone on my shoulder. "I barely got in the door. What's up?"

"When you're chasing a big-time thief, why wait?"

I nod. "Good point."

"Well, here's what I've got, or more concisely, what I haven't got. I called the personnel office at O'Hare and they were not willing to talk to me on the phone. So, in that sense I have nothing. There was a tone in the director's voice that told me she knew something and really did want to share. That's a big leap but that's what my experience tells me."

"I trust your judgement about that. Let me think about what our next step ought to be. I'll be back to you soon."

What I didn't want to tell him was that while I trust his judgment that there is something there, I'm not ready to go so far as sending him out to Chicago. I don't expect Allen will buy that right now, either. But I decide to check it out with him.

I get him on his cell and tell him the story.

"Patrick, I think it's worth following up but, no," he says, "I won't trust anyone to do that but you. Make the arrangements yourself and fly out there and see what you can learn."

"You got it. Later."

I figure because the personnel director is on the airport

premises, I will able to catch a morning flight, talk to her and return to Boston the same day. I won't even think about leaving Gineen alone overnight, even with nurses standing by.

CHAPTER VIII

I call United and explore schedules with the clerk. I finally settle on an early morning flight that leaves Logan at 6:50 a.m. and arrives at O'Hare at about 11:30, and a return flight that leaves Chicago at 2:30 in the afternoon and gets back at 7:30. That gives me about three hours at O'Hare, which should be enough, given the personnel office is on the airport property. I book the flights for tomorrow morning. Next, I call Sam at his home and he picks up.

"Sam, this is Patrick. Feel free to turn me down but I must get to Logan Airport tomorrow morning for a 5:50 a.m. flight. If that's too early for you, I can certainly find someone else to cart me out there in the middle of the night."

"Don't be silly. I'll be glad to pick you up. No problem at all for me. Tomorrow is my day off and I have nothing planned. Just to be on the safe side, let's leave an hour. I'll pick you up at quarter to five. Even at that hour of the morning, traffic through the tunnels can be brutal."

I hang up the phone and leave my office. On the first floor, I find Fran, and explain the situation.

"Fran, I am going to make an emergency trip to Chicago early tomorrow morning. I've arranged it, so I will be back around eight. Why don't you sleep upstairs in the guest room, and I will sack out down here? I'll try not to make any noise in the morning. Gineen doesn't know I am going to be away, so let her know it's a last minute thing and that I will be back in the evening."

"You needn't worry about anything. Just go ahead and do you work," she says. "Cynthia and I will take care of everything."

"With you two here, I won't worry about anything. So good to have you both."

"Oh pish-posh, just doing our job like you are. See you tomorrow night. I'm sure you will excuse me, but I won't be up at that ungodly hour to see you off. Good night now."

I am up and dressed when Sam arrives right on time.

"Good morning, Sam," I greet him, slipping into the cab. "How are you?"

"Considering the hour, I'm fine. Where are you off to?"

"Chicago. Head for United's terminal. I don't want to leave Gineen alone overnight so I'm coming back tonight."

"Perfect. Tell me when and I'll be here to take you home."

When we get to Logan, I give him the return flight information and then head for the check-in desk.

The fight is uneventful, and we arrive on time. Since I'm without any luggage, I head straight for a phone and call the personnel director's office.

"Good morning, my name is Patrick Ingel, an investigator from Boston. May I speak to Stacey Morgan, please?"

"Mr. Ingel, this is Stacey's assistant, Joanne, and I was the one who talked to your partner yesterday. I didn't expect to hear from you so soon. Fortunately, Stacey is in this morning. She's talking to one of our employees right now. Come on over. It won't be a long wait."

I am in luck; I walk over to the office.

It's a short wait until a nicely dressed, attractive woman comes out of her office and extends her hand. I take it and offer, "Miss Morgan," I say after glancing at her bare left hand, "good of you to see me on such short notice."

"No problem," she says pleasantly. "Come on into my office."

As we sit down, I am the first to talk. "I don't really know where to begin," I say. "It's a very short story and quite frankly, I am here on a fishing expedition. Elvin Ponce is employed by my client back in Massachusetts as a security guard. He seems harmless, although he was on duty when a large theft took place. I have a hard time believing he was involved in any way, but as you probably know, looks can often be deceiving. He was on guard duty at the time. Hard to see how he could have missed it, but it could have been he was at the john or some other place. That's about all I know about him."

"How well I know that problem," she says, grinning. "Elvin was employed here for several years in several different job categories. If could summarize his performance, there is only one word – incompetent. I had to *separate* him, to use a kind word, and he left several months ago. He lived in the village of Elk Grove not far from here and in a house owned and inhabited by his mother. Because of all the valuable cargo and passengers passing through the airport, we do a very thorough background check before we hire anyone."

"I'm not surprised by that," I say and jot down some notes. "Was there any hint whatsoever about theft or any other criminal acts?"

"Well this is an airport and we have a continuing problem with missing cargo, but we never had any evidence that

Ponce was involved."

"It doesn't make sense to bother you any further. Thank you so much for your time."

"No bother at all. Are you going back to Boston today?"

I am tempted to ask her to lunch but decide against it. "Yes, I am. My wife is receiving cancer treatments and although she has round the clock nursing care, I don't want to be away overnight."

"I'm sorry to hear that," she says solemnly. "I wish her good luck and you too."

"Thanks."

I leave her office and walk on over to a restaurant in the terminal. I get seated by a large window where I can watch the steady parade of incoming and outgoing planes. I can't get on an earlier flight, so I've got a couple of hours to kill before I leave. Whipping out my ever-present notebook, I start making notes about where I go next. Certainly, I'm not finished with Ponce but I'm not exactly sure where to go with him. Maybe I'll put Marshall on him. His instincts are good, and I have other places and things to do. We're just scratching the surface. My flight is called on time. I luck out with another uneventful flight which gets in right on schedule. Sam meets me in the terminal. We find his cab and I'm back home just before eight. When I get there, Cynthia tells me that Gineen has eaten a light dinner and has tolerated it very well.

"She's asleep upstairs and is comfortable." Nurse-talk for don't disturb her.

"I'm just going to tip toe upstairs and take quick look, and then come back down here to sleep."

"OK then. We're next store and available any time as you

know. Have a good night."

"You too. See you in the morning."

I go quietly up the carpeted stairs and peek through the door which is opened a crack. Like Cynthia said, Gineen is sound asleep, breathing slowly and deeply. I stare for a few moments thinking how good this makes me feel. This has been a very long day for me, so I curl up on the sleep sofa downstairs and fall asleep myself. I have vivid dreams all night long. My sleep is interrupted by a tickling sensation. When I try to scratch it, I realize it is Gineen's lovely black hair that is swinging back and forth over my face.

"Hello big fella. I thought you'd never wake up. I thought I'd speed things up a bit, so we can spend a little alone time before the nurse team marches in."

The combined sweet aroma of her hair and body odors wake me up fast. "I'm up. I'm up, but should we be doing this?"

"Remember, I have cancer, not the measles or leprosy. You make love to me right now or I'll report you to the SPCHW. That's the Society for the Prevention of Cruelty to Horny Women to ill-informed lowlifes like you."

I give in and she leads me through her entire love routine after which we both fall sound asleep. It is only five o'clock when she stirs and wakes me up.

"The early bird really does get the worm, doesn't she?"

"Now get up and make me some breakfast or I'll tell Cynthia and Franny that you molested me."

"Shouldn't we wait for them to tell us what you can eat?"

"No, it's OK. I'm a big girl. Make me a couple of soft scrambled eggs and a slice of toast. Trust me. I can handle it. Y'know, I have another round of chemo coming up and I could use some strength to get through it."

I begrudgingly follow her wishes, all the while hoping I'm doing the right thing. Her breakfast disappears in just a few minutes and then she turns to me and issues one more order. "Now do the dishes while I go up and shower."

I am just about ready to protest when the doorbell rings and in marches Cynthia. I tell her about breakfast and ask if I did the right thing to which she responds, "Of course you did. She knows what her system can handle better than we do."

"She told me that she has another round of chemo coming up. When is that?"

"Tomorrow or the day after. We will check in with her doc today."

"Oh, by the way, sorry to meet you in my jammies but I'm getting ready to take a shower when Gineen is done."

"Oh really?" said with a slight grin.

"I'll get to the dishes now, if you will excuse me."

"Go right ahead. I'll wait for Gineen in the living room."

I clean up the kitchen and follow Gineen to the shower. When I am dressed and heading for the office to do some work, the two of them catch me in the living room. "Hey detective," Gineen says, "we are going out for a walk."

"Good, I'll see you when you get back. The exercise will be good for you."

"No, no dummy for you. Running around on airplanes and sitting in your office is not exercise, so come along with us to the Emerald Necklace and put on your running shoes."

Off we go with Gineen setting the pace, Cynthia and I following. After about a mile or so, she starts to slow, and I trot up alongside her. "Hey," I say, "are you overdoing it?"

"Yeah. I am getting a little winded and a bit nauseous."

I pull her over to a bench and make her sit down.

"It's OK," she says. "I just need a little rest."

"Sure."

I put my arm around her and feel a slight shudder. When that subsides, I suggest, "Let's walk back to the condo now. We've had enough for today."

"I overdid it a bit, but relax, I'm OK," she says with an edge in her voice. "Give me another minute and we can go back."

We make it back to the condo without any further trouble. When we get there, she says to me, "I'm going upstairs to rest. Please don't worry. I'm fine. Just tired. Go do some work."

Up the stairs she goes without any help. When she's upstairs and can't hear, I turn to the nurses and give them a questioning look as I raise my arms, palms up.

"Patrick," says Franny, "she's teaching herself her limits as only she can do. She'll be fine, so do what she says and go find some work."

"OK, if you say so." I am so concerned about Gineen's health that when I sit down at my desk I do absolutely nothing for a half an hour except doodle on my pad. The ringing of the telephone brings me out of my reverie.

"Hello, Patrick Ingel here."

"Good morning Ingel, this is Allen. I thought I'd check with you about the results of your trip to Chicago. How are you?"

"I'm OK but a little off target. My wife had an attack of nausea a short while ago and I'm so worried about her that I need some time to get back in step."

"No problem. Nothing's more important than family. I hope she is OK."

"She will be. Can we talk on the phone after lunch or would you rather get together later in the afternoon?"

"Phone of course. I'll call you. Please give your wife my best. Bye."

"Bye."

Back to doodling and thinking. I am a bit more focused now. I imagine that Mr. Ponce should be at the top of my list. He clearly needs more work and is the only one who has earned that. Maybe just a question of incompetency as suggested by his former employer. Maybe not. Should I do the background check and maybe confront him? Or would Marshall be a better fit? Given my distraction with Gineen, I would be happy to palm it off on him. My good sense tells me that Allen would not be happy with that, so I jot down my questions.

I. Where did he work prior to O'Hare? Why did he leave that job?

2. Why did he leave the O'Hare job?

3. What brought him to Brandt's mansion?

4. What is his address?

5. Who owns the place if it is a condo or single family?

6. Does he have any sources of income outside of the salary Brandt pays him? How much is that?

7. May I see his driver's license? What kind of a car does he drive? Year?

8. Does he have any career aspirations? How long will he work for Brandt?

9. Has he ever had any criminal complaints lodged against him? Civil Complaints? Outcomes?

10. Married? Children? Other relatives in the Boston area? Names, addresses, etc.

11. Did he know Brandt or any of his employees prior to coming here to work?

12. Why did he decide to work for Brandt?

13. How did he know Brandt was looking for a security guard?

14. Will he submit to a lie detector test?

15. Has he spoken to any attorney about anything since coming here? Ever?

16. Does he understand why I am asking these questions?

Late in the afternoon, Allen calls and I go over the list of questions I have compiled to lay on Ponce. He agrees I should focus first on Ponce, and, as I suspected, he wants me to do the work and not Marshall.

"I don't mean to put pressure on you, but fairness dictates that we formally respond to Brandt's claim within a reasonable timeframe."

"And that would be what?"

"Each case is different, and the size of this loss is so large that we have some leeway. For the sake of argument let's set our sights on thirty days. OK with you?"

"Shouldn't take that long to come up with the thief or just call it quits."

"OK then. Go to work, Ingel, and keep in touch. Again, my regards to your wife and wishes for a speedy and complete recovery."

"Got it, Allen."

Gineen gets up at five and comes downstairs looking a bit pale but not as bad as I expected. Fran and Cynthia have gone back to Roger's condo, so I assume the chef's role. I hug her and ask, "Do you think you can have a little chicken soup for dinner?"

"That would be good. I still have some nausea but not so bad. Chicken soup would be fine. Are you going to make it from scratch?

"Yeah, sure. I made the original recipe and sold it to Campbell's some years ago."

"Imagine, a first-class chef with such a poor sense of humor. Bring it on, maestro."

"Notice how expertly I open the can and pour the contents into the pan without spilling a drop."

"Enough, jerk face. Turn the burner on so I can eat before daybreak."

"Jerk face? You are so cruel."

"Cruel? Nah. Wait until I am strong enough to land a left jab. That will be cruel. Aren't you gonna eat?"

"I didn't want to eat some good stuff in front of you," I say. "That would indeed be cruel."

"I can handle it. Go make yourself something. At the rate I am sipping, I won't be done until nine o'clock."

I whip up a thick juicy hamburger and some home fries. Well, the hamburger came already prepared from the supermarket, but the potatoes are leftovers that I made myself. The final touch is a fat slice of onion for the burger and a bottle of cold beer. I slink into the dining room with my dinner, still feeling some pangs of guilt. I start to eat without looking directly at Gineen.

"Hey detective, do you suppose you could find a napkin? There's ketchup running down your chin."

"Now you are the one being cruel," I say, reaching for a napkin. "You are an old meanie."

"Poor baby. Wipe your chin and your shirt and mommy will give you a kiss and make everything better. Anymore ketchup on you and you'll need a shower."

I get my kiss and we both have a small laugh at the great ketchup spill of 2016.

"Bigger story than the 1918 Great Molasses Spill in the north end," she quips and I laugh with her.

The mood has now softened, and we hug, kiss, and hike up to the bedroom where we cuddle until sleep takes over.

At breakfast in the morning, I let Gineen know that I am going out to Brandt's mansion to do some work. "I should be back in a few hours," I say. "I'll knock on Fran's door and let her know I am leaving."

"You go and do some good work. I'm rested this morning. Still feeling the aftereffects of last night's laughter. Thank you for being with me and understanding. I love you dearly and forever."

"Aw. I don't deserve you."

"You're right about that. Now, get out."

On the way out to Brandt's, I try to organize my thoughts which I outlined yesterday. I don't call and announce my trip. A frontal attack seems best to me, but I can almost guarantee that it won't work. When I drive up to the gate, Ponce lets me in and instead of proceeding on to the house, I stop and get out of the car.

"Good morning, Mr. Ponce," I say politely. "I'm glad you're on duty this morning because I came out to ask you a few questions."

"About what, Mr. Ingel? I've already told you what I know about the jewel theft."

"This is more about you than the theft."

"I don't know, Mr. Ingel," he says, rubbing his neck. "I think you should talk to Swazey about that."

There you go. I knew he wouldn't talk to me unless ordered to by his boss.

At the mansion, I am met at the door by Swazey.

"Good morning, Mr. Ingel. I didn't know you had an appointment today."

"I don't, Swazey," I admit. "I came out to talk to Ponce, your security guard, and he sent me up here."

"What in the world did he do that for? Talk to him all you want about the theft."

"What I want from him isn't directly about the jewelry theft but more about his background."

"Oh, goodness. Do you have some reason to suspect he was involved?"

"No, but as I told both you and Brandt – everyone is a suspect until it is clear they had nothing to do with it."

"Well, I certainly want to talk to Mr. Brandt before you go any further with Mr. Ponce."

"Well, go right ahead and ask him."

"I'm sorry, but Mr. Brandt has not yet shown up for breakfast."

"Well, dammit, go wake him," I say shortly. "It's 9:30 and if he wants any progress made on his claim, he'd better talk to me right now."

"Yes, sir. I will see if he's up right now."

They make me wait another ten minutes and finally Brandt shows up, impeccably dressed. Obviously, he's been up for a while.

"Mr. Ingel, Swazey tells me you are anxious to talk to me. What can I do for you today?"

"Well you don't need to do anything at all, except make your security guard available."

"I'd be glad to do that. We have three, you know. Which one would you like to see or perhaps all of them?"

"Mr. Brandt, you are giving me a hard time and if you'd like I'll discontinue my investigation, which means there will be no action taken on your claim," I bark. "Now, either produce Mr. Ponce who is outside at the gate or I leave."

"I am most certainly cooperating with you and your company. I resent any insinuations to the contrary."

"I am not insinuating. I am stating a fact."

"If you must. Swazey, go out and bring Ponce in here."

"No way! I will talk to him out there...alone."

"Go right ahead. Rest assured that I will be in touch with Mr. Allen to let him know of your rude behavior and threats."

"Go right ahead. Here let me give you his phone number. Would you like me to call him right now?"

"Just go do your alleged work and leave the premises."

I don't acknowledge his order and walk back out to the gate. When I get there, I see Ponce just getting off the phone. Undoubtedly a call from Brandt.

"Getting your orders from Mr. Brandt?"

"Oh yessir. He told me to cooperate fully with you."

"I'll bet. Let me start at the beginning. I know your last job before coming here was at O'Hare. Where did you work before that?"

He looks up at the sky and rubs his chin as if this is a very difficult question. Finally, he says, "I believe that would have been in Las Vegas."

"You believe?" I ask, my patience running thin. "Aren't you sure?"

"Yes, I'm sure."

"And where did you work there and what kind of work did

you do?"

"I worked at the Sands Casino as a security guard."

"For how long?" I put pen to paper.

"For about five years."

"And what was your salary there?"

"When I left, about $40,000 a year."

"Pretty good for a security job," I say, watching his eyes. "Did you work inside the casino or outside?"

"Inside, sir. I was a roving guard and covered all of the gambling operations at one time or another."

"Why did you leave such a good job?" I ask, jotting down more thoughts.

"Why, sir, Mr. Brandt offered me a better opportunity," he says.

"Are you telling me your salary here is more than $40,000?"

"No. I'm not. I took a $10,000 cut to come here."

I stop writing and look up at him. "What was the attraction?"

"Why, sir, the opportunity for advancement," he says. "I was told I could be in line for Swazey's job in a few years."

"And that salary is how much?"

"Sir, I think you should ask Swazey that question."

"I'm asking you."

"I don't know for a fact, but I'm pretty sure it's around $50,000."

"Mr. Brandt pays well."

"Yes." Ponce nods. "He does."

"And how did Brandt find you? Or did you find him?"

"You could say we found each other."

"Nonsense. Please be more specific."

"Well, I answered an advertisement he placed on a website

devoted to job opportunities."

"See that didn't hurt. Did it?" I ask a few more innocuous questions and he produces his driver's license, his one credit card, and his address. "What kind of a car do you drive?"

"A Chevy pickup truck. I don't have a passenger car." I ask for and he produces the vehicles' registration and insurance card.

"Is there a loan outstanding on this vehicle?"

"No." This is an expensive, top of the line Chevrolet 150 truck of very current vintage. I make a mental note to explore this further after he says it was purchased new at the local Chevy dealer.

"Do you have any other sources of income other than the salary that Brandt pays you?"

"Not really. I do have a small retirement annuity from my Las Vegas job, but the income is automatically reinvested, so I don't see any of it."

Switching subjects quickly. "Did you know any of Brandt's employees before you came here?"

"No."

"Do you rent or own the place where you live?"

"I rent a small condo for $900 a month. Can't afford to buy anything." He offers this too smoothly and I wonder just what he can afford. "Which local banks do you do business with?"

"Just one, the TD Bank nearby. Checking and savings both. There is a total of about $3,000 combined in both."

I'm starting to distrust this guy since he is going out of his way to show me how little money he has. Here is where I slip in the shocker, "Are you willing to take a lie detector test?"

"Are you accusing me of lying? Am I a suspect in the

Brandt theft?"

"Of course, you are. Everyone in the vicinity is until I find the real thieves."

"I don't know about a lie detector test. Maybe I should talk to a lawyer before I do that."

"Maybe you should." I have no intention of attempting to give him a lie detector test, but his reaction suggests to me that he is hiding something. I don't know what, but he deserves some further work, particularly on his financial assets.

"Thanks for your help," I say. "Why don't you go back to work? Call Swazey back and let him know that I'm done."

After leaving Ponce, I drive to Dunkin Donuts, buy a couple of donuts and a black coffee and sit down to thinks things over. Outside of a nagging suspicion about Ponce, I am getting nowhere fast on this job and I am starting to have doubts that I will ever solve it. What could Ponce be hiding? A relationship with the jewelry thieves? Maybe. A hidden stash of cash? Maybe. If it is money, it could be a link to Brandt; a payoff for helping with the theft. Maybe so but how can I find it? It could be anywhere in the world. Stumped. My head starts to hurt so it's back to the condo just in time for lunch.

Fran is just preparing a light lunch for Gineen. I know she is scheduled for another round of chemo tomorrow, so they are especially careful with her intake today.

"Well if it isn't the brightest detective in town," Gineen says from her spot at the table. "And how did it go today?"

"I'm going nowhere on this job and its starting to get me down."

"What you need is a nice big lunch."

"Well, err, I'm not too hungry yet."

"Not too hungry? What do you mean? It's already past your normal lunch time. Oh, I get it; you had lunch out."

"Not exactly. Just some coffee and a few donuts."

"Bad boy. I should have known. What's really on your mind?"

I need to bounce a few questions off her pretty and smart head. I tell her about my interview with Ponce.

She thinks for a minute and then offers a suggestion. "Your next step is rather obvious, my man," she says. "Just go out to his condo and see what you can find."

"What are you suggesting Gineen? That I sweet talk myself into the condo?"

"No silly, break in. You know, jimmy the lock."

"And do you think Ponce is dumb enough to have left a road map of his exploits lying around?"

"God, you are slow today. Must be the donuts. You won't know what you are looking for until you get inside. Don't worry, breaking and entering is not a big offense, particularly for a first timer. Besides we'll bail you out of jail before too much time passes. After all, we need someone here to take out the garbage."

"Funny. But maybe I'll give it a try."

"What maybe? Get out there now, since you know Ponce is at the mansion. Go and do."

"I'm on my way. I knew there was a reason to talk to you. I haven't been arrested for breaking and entering in a long time. Bye."

I find Ponce's condo which is one of a four-unit building.

My first break is that his is on the ground floor. The second break is that the units have decks in the rear, out of sight of neighbors and the last one is that there is a sliding glass door providing access to the interior of the condo. A piece of cake for an experienced detective like me. So, I quickly get inside with the help of a simple pick.

I stop, half expecting a roommate to shoot me. Nope. No one there. There is a small kitchen, a small bedroom and living room-combination office, equipped with a computer. I know I won't be able to get into it, but I tap the mouse anyhow, and lo and behold it takes me to a list of contacts. After hurriedly copying the list, I scoot out of there and back to my car the same way I came in. When I get back to the condo and report what I think is a great coup, I am met with disdain from Gineen.

"Are you telling me you didn't copy the entire contents of his computer while you were there? Now you have to go back and do just that."

"Wait a minute. Are you suggesting I break and enter a second time in the same day? After all, my knowledge of computers is basic, and I wouldn't even know how to copy the damn thing."

"It's easy and I will show you how right now. Come into the office."

She shows me how and I do head back to Ponce's condo. When I arrive, his pickup truck is parked in the driveway, so I am saved from a second breaking and entering escapade. At least for today.

"Back already master detective," Gineen greets when I return to the condo. "That was fast. Let's see what you have. Bring that disc in here."

"Can't do. Ponce was already back at the house."

"And you let a little thing like that stop you?"

"Your comedy routine is getting just a bit stale, to put it in printable words. And I now realize that it will not be a good idea to go back into his house at all. I get caught and it's the end of the line for me as a P.I. Ponce is not the dumb, incompetent security guard I once thought he was. Maybe a little sloppy for leaving his computer on but he probably didn't expect an honest investigator like me to break into his house. I'm going to focus on the information I have from that escapade, namely the list of contacts. You know, now that I think back, the packing box to that computer was still in the room. Suggests to me that it was new and maybe there wasn't anything on it besides the contacts. Possibly he was just using it for emailing his buddies. In any event, I am not going back in there, at least not until I have explored the contacts list. I suggest you rest up now and get ready for tomorrow's chemo."

"I'll take you up on that but let me know how things go. Thinking about your case will take my mind off the chemo. OK?"

"Of course. No problem. I'll need some time, but I promise to let you in on my little secret, if I ever get one."

"I have faith. Later."

My mind is spinning around like a tire slipping on a glare ice surface. Soon, I calm down and start to reason things out. I jot some notes down as a beginning. The list of contacts starts with two familiar names, Swazey and Brandt. No surprise there. The man works for them. The other two mean nothing to me. Ahmadi and Karzai. They are clearly names of a foreign origin. My Toshiba tells me that they are both of

Afghani origin. My mind leaps to the likely substance behind these names. DRUGS! Afghanistan being a prime source for drugs coming into the states. Two guys, one probably based in Afghanistan to ship, and one in this country to pick up and distribute. A good theory but how do I substantiate it? Why it's obvious, I will check in with the brains in the family. For now, I let her rest until I wake her for dinner.

"My, my, you were really dead to the world."

"Not a good choice of words for a cancer patient, Patrick," she says. "It seems like I already suggested to you once to pick some more appropriate phrases. You can be such a slow learner for a supposedly savvy private investigator."

Changing the subject quickly, I respond, "Can I get you something to eat?"

"Something light."

"How about Jewish Penicillin? Chicken soup."

"Some Jew you are, Patrick. Sure. Go ahead and open the can if you can find the can opener."

"Actually, I was prepared to make it from scratch."

"That would be a good trick. We don't have any chicken, lover."

"Oh yeah. Where did you say the can opener was?"

"Lord. In the top draw to the left of the sink. You think you will need any help with that job?"

"I detect a note of sarcasm so I don't know if I will share my little secret with you as I planned to do."

"Spare me. Let's eat and then you can share whatever you want."

We eat slowly and I clean up the place while Gineen relaxes in the living room. When my housekeeping chores are done, I find her in our large rocking chair.

"OK, sweet wonderful woman, let's get to the recent inroads to my investigation. There are two names in Ponce's list of contacts in addition to Brandt and Swazey. They are both Afghani names. I theorize that they are parts of a drug smuggling operation since Afghanistan is a large producer of drugs. That's about as far as I have gotten, so the next step would be to follow up on these two and see where that leads."

"Yeah. And so?"

"Well, that's where you come in since I know almost nothing about how to manipulate the damn computer."

"Simpler to go brake into Ponce's place and download the contents of his computer."

"Don't want to do that if we can avoid it. Why don't you call up some of your IT magic and see what we can learn without me chancing a jail term for breaking and entering? The surnames of the two contacts are Ahmadi and Karzai. Is there any way you can get background information on these two guys?"

"If there is any data out there, I can get it, but the price is high,"

"C'mon woman This is close to a matter of life and death. Isn't it you who chides me about sarcasm?"

"Good point. Let me see what I can find out. Go for a fifteen minute walk while I work. You're so handsome, you distract me."

It's a warm day and I walk up to Coolidge Corner and back, all the while thinking how I got into this mess and where it might be taking me. I will refuse to go to Afghanistan. For sure. When I get back to the condo, Gineen has a twinkle in her eyes and a bit of a smirk on her face.

"Well, pretty boy, I cracked this question wide open like an elephant stomping on a walnut."

"And?"

"And it's just like you thought, one guy in Afghanistan. Really in Peshawar, Pakistan, just on the border with Afghanistan. The other one is in California. San Francisco to be exact."

"I understand that Peshawar is a great place to shop. Why don't you take that one and I'll go to the west coast?"

"Funny. For some reason, I doubt that either one of us, or even the CIA, can find much on him, so I'll pass on that trip, funny man."

CHAPTER X

Early the next morning, I am on the phone with Allen to bring him up to date.

"Good morning, Allen."

"Good morning, Ingel. What's up? Progress, I hope."

"Haven't solved the case yet, but I do have a pregnant lead to check out."

"And what is that?"

"The case is turning into one with international implications," I explain. "When we checked out the list of contacts on Ponce's computer, we found two names of Afghani origin. One on our west coast, and one on the Pakistan-Afghanistan border in Peshawar. That leads me to suspect that we are likely taking about a drug connection."

"Do you have any hard evidence of this? And if so, what is the connection with Ponce?"

"You are way out in front of me. No, we do not have any hard evidence except the Afghani names on Ponce's computer. In truth, we don't even have that since I got the contacts from his computer by...er, well, breaking and entering his apartment."

I hold my breath for a minute, expecting to be fired after this admission. Not a peep from Allen so I continue, "We need a way to get some information about the California guy whose name is Karzai."

"And I'm guessing you have found a way to do that."

"Well, I think so. Before we came to Boston, I worked with a clerk in the Connecticut Motor Vehicle Department who was good at obtaining out of state drivers' licenses. It just so happens she is now apparently having a fling with Roger Jones, from the Casino."

"Well, if she's OK with you and OK with Roger, there is no doubt in my mind that she can be discreet, so get in touch with her."

"OK, I will."

"You are doing a good job, but I wish the problem wasn't getting so complicated. Keep me up to date. Maybe we should turn the case over to the State Department or the CIA. Just joking. It's our problem, at least for the time being. Later."

By the time I'm finished with Allen, Gineen is up and dressed.

"Good morning, my princess. Do you feel as good as you look?"

"I feel good right now and I hope I'll feel as good at the end of the day."

'You're talking about your chemo dose. Yes?"

"I am. Don't think I'm getting to be a wimp, but could you hang around today? I might need someone to hug and Franny just doesn't fit the bill."

"Why I'm flattered. I shall be here all day. One of the things I will be working on is trying to track down an Afghani who lives in California. I think you and I may have stumbled onto an international drug ring, which is connected to Mr. Ponce."

"What do you mean us, pale face? I was the one who led you to their names."

"But I was the one who broke into Ponce's house, risking my life or jail to get the names off his computer. Don't I get a little credit?"

"Yes, just a little. You are the effective crook and I am the brilliant IT analyst. That's how it will play out when we make a movie out of it."

"Not to change the subject, but are you having your chemo before or after lunch?"

"After. Franny thinks it would be easier on my system if there was food in my belly before I take the cursed stuff."

"Let me whip you up a feast of your favorite tofu salad."

"Such a dear man. I take back almost all the shitty things, I've said about you in the last couple of years. Nevertheless, you are still my slave. Understood?"

"Yes, mistress. Now off to the kitchen with me!"

"Gee whiz, Gineen, I can only find enough tofu for one serving," I say coyly while standing in the kitchen. "What a disaster. Now I'll have to settle for a cheeseburger."

"I don't believe I've ever seen you eat tofu. Maybe, one of these days you could try it."

"I'll put it on my list."

"Right. Go make your cheeseburger. You should consider the fact that tofu is said to act like an enhancer to sexual performance."

"Now who's being funny?"

After lunch, Franny comes in and gives her the dose of chemo. She reacts rather well initially but I know it is difficult predicting how long that will last. I hug and kiss her, and she goes upstairs to rest, while I go into the office to call Sally Langone. I have worked with Sally in the past, long before she took up with Roger. I luck out and get her at her condo on the first try. "Hello Sally, this is Patrick. How are you?"

"Oh, I'm just fine but more importantly, how is Gineen doing?"

"Thanks for asking. She is taking the chemotherapy reasonably well, but there is a price to pay. She's a trooper and doesn't complain."

"Good it's no picnic for either of you but I just know it will turn out just fine."

"I hope so, but you are right, it's hard for me to stand by and know that she is having a really tough time. I get away from it sometimes to work on the investigation of a jewel theft. That reminds me to ask a favor from you. I have two characters who are somehow involved with the theft. One of them I know is named Karzai and he lives in California but that's all I know. I thought you might be able to get a copy of his driver's license and whatever else about his background you can find. His name is clearly Afghani in origin. The second one is way out of your jurisdiction, and I don't need to know anything about him. He lives somewhere in Pakistan or Afghanistan."

"Wow! Somewhere far out is right. Don't have any connections in Afghanistan. The other one should be a piece of cake, particularly with his unusual name. I'll get back to you as soon as I can. Shouldn't take very long. Is tomorrow soon enough? I'm seeing Roger tonight for dinner and I need to get my hair done this afternoon."

"Not a problem, Sally. By the way my client will be happy to pay your usual fee."

"Nonsense. Consider it a small token of my feelings for you two. Besides I'm not doing that kind of stuff anymore and I'm on the verge of getting out of it for good."

This thing with Roger sounds like it is very serious. Indeed, like I suspected.

"Sally, if you guys tie the knot, Gineen and I will be expecting an invitation. After all, you two were at our ceremony, and you both feel like family to us."

"We're not there yet but in all honesty, we are heading in that direction. Call you back tomorrow."

When I finish the call, Gineen comes downstairs, looking pale and tired. After a hug and a kiss, I say to her, "Hello, beautiful."

"Patrick. I just looked in the bathroom mirror. I know how I look. Don't snow me."

"OK, you look tired and pale, but you still are the loveliest woman in Boston."

"Stop with the Irish blarney."

"It's true. Hey, I just had a call from Sally Langone and she sends her love,"

"Really? How is she doing?"

"Well, good. She sounded happy and she talked about retiring from the state. It sounds like she and Roger are moving closer and closer to a permanent relationship. I told her if they did get married, we'd be disappointed if we didn't get invited."

"That's terrific."

"She did agree to do one more search for me and she'll be calling me back sometime tomorrow with everything she could find out regarding our Afghani friend, Karzai. Now, the bad news. Someone is going to have to go out to California and check into this guy. Allen wants me to do it, but I really don't want to. No telling how long it will take but the round-trip flight itself will consume the best part of two days."

"Pardon me for interrupting but I can read you like an open book and you are trying to protect me. Go out there and do your job. Let's have a happy time for the rest of the day. OK?"

"No ten jobs are worth more than you. If you're certain it's OK, I'll think about going."

"Haven't I always been honest with you? And besides I have Cynthia and Franny, so stop worrying. Please."

"It's a deal if you promise to stop punching me every time you feel like it."

"No can do."

We watch a couple of chick flicks and go to bed early since Gineen is exhausted. In the morning, I catch Franny before Gineen wakes up. "Franny, I am probably going to California tomorrow or the next day. I have misgivings about that but Gineen insists that I go. Promise me that you will call me on my cell immediately if there is any change in her condition."

"I'll do that but understand she is probably going to feel punky for some time, whether you are here or not. She is a tough cookie and takes it well, so go do your job and relax. She is in good hands."

"I know and thank both of you for taking such good care of her."

"It's our job."

Late in the morning, I get a call from Sally. She tells me she has tracked down Karzai in San Francisco.

"Take down this address. It's in Bernal Heights."

I make a note of it and start looking at airline flights from Logan airport.

CHAPTER XI

Next morning bright and early I tip toe into the bedroom after my shower and kiss Gineen lightly on the forehead, not meaning to awaken her.

"Good morning, detective. Are you off to San Francisco already?"

"Sorry. I didn't mean to wake you. I called Sam Jones last night and arranged for him to pick me up at seven, so he can get to Logan by eight."

"Naughty boy. You were going to leave without waking me, weren't you?"

"Yeah. You know how I hate to wake you. You need your sleep."

"I need your love more than I need sleep. One more kiss and go do your job as Bill Belichick always says. And say hello to Sam for me."

"I will. Franny is already downstairs. You take care and call me if you need anything. I'll only be five hours away."

With that I'm out the door as Sam is already waiting. "Can I take that bag for you?" he offers.

"Cut it out, Sam," I answer, as I throw the bag in the back seat. "American Airlines terminal."

On the way there, I ask Sam to stop in once a day and check with the nurses while I'm gone and make sure that Gineen is OK. "And call me on my cell. I'm nervous leaving her alone even with the nurses there."

"No problem. I'll be sure to do that and get them whatever they might need, as well."

"Thanks, Sam. You are a good friend."

"Bah. Nothing. That's what friends are for. Here we are. You have a good flight and a successful trip."

I go through all the necessary security checks and walk quickly to the gate. I had already taken the precaution of leaving my handgun at home, since I knew I could not get it on board without lots of work. Maybe not at all. I'm travelling first class and have a good breakfast and a pleasant trip on Allen's tab. Five hours later, we land at San Francisco International Airport after a smooth and uneventful flight. I snoozed rather than watched a movie. Once on the ground, I go to the Budget car rental and get a Japanese hybrid, so I can move quietly around the city. Just in case quiet is necessary. It's relatively inconspicuous in this city of hybrids. I drive into the city and rent a room downtown at the Hilton Park Hotel in Union Square. The location is not as close to Bernal Heights as I would like, but that's life in the big city.

Because of the time change from the east coast, it is still early in the day, so I drive out to the address that Sally gave me, which is 207 Elsie Street. As I drive by, I note that the house is a narrow one on a steep street but there are no parking spaces within view that I can squeeze into. I circle around a few times and find one out of sight of the house. By the look of the area it may be three days before I find a suitable space, where I can sit in the car and watch the house. I walk on by it to learn what I can. I don't have any idea how I am going to approach the problem, except with caution since this guy Karzai will have huge resources available, if he really is the large importer of drugs that I think he is. I start out overmatched and I know it, so forewarned is fore armed. I hope.

I walk up the hill past the house and then turn around and walk back by it again. The house has a narrow off-street drive that slopes downward away from the street with no cars parked in it. To the left as I face the house, there is a flight of stairs up to the first floor, which is above street level. There isn't a car parked in the driveway. Even if there were, I wouldn't know if it was Karzai's. I need one more favor from Sally and until then I decide to call it quits. Back at the hotel, I call Sally.

"Sally, I wouldn't ask you this and should have asked before. So please excuse me."

"Pish posh, it's nothing, dear boy. Ask away."

"I need to know information on Karzai's automobile, so I can ID it and if you can get it, any information on the registered history of the vehicle."

"Piece of cake. I'll get back to you within a few hours."

"Thanks, Sally."

I have some time and it is San Francisco, so I take out my tourist guide and walk to Lombard Street. Incredible. I don't believe what I'm seeing. It's famous for having eight hairpin turns within the space of one block. I have a faint memory of seeing it in a movie, but in real life it is fantastic especially to a New England Yankee like me. I think to myself that it would be interesting to find out the history of how it came into existence. After that, I take a short ride on a cable car and I know I have seen this piece of antiquity in more than one movie. Back at the hotel I have a Bushmills and soda while waiting for Sally to call. She does, shortly before dinner.

"Hi, Patrick. Sorry this took a bit longer than I thought it would."

"It's OK. I played tourist this afternoon. San Francisco is a fantastic city. Some of it reminds me of Boston but based on what I've seen so far, it has a bit too much flash for me and far too many tourists."

"In other words, nice place to visit but you wouldn't like to live there."

"Nah. What have you found for me?"

"Karzai has not one but two Mercedes cars. A plain one-year-old sedan and a flashy sport vehicle. Take down these tag numbers."

I write them down on a small scratch pad that I always carry with me. "Are they both registered in his name?"

"No, the sedan is registered in his wife's name and the sports car is in his. I found out that he previously had a small economy sedan registered to him in Alameda, not very far from the seaport. It was sold about two years ago."

"Sounds like he won the lottery. Or something."

"Oh, and before that he lived outside the country, in Afghanistan. I hope this information is helpful, but I believe it's the end of the line for me. I have no contacts in Afghanistan."

"Probably a good thing. Sally, thank you so much. I owe you dinner when you and Roger come to Boston."

"I'll take you up on that. Love to Gineen. Bye now."

Looks like my drug theory guess is locked in tight. I have dinner in the hotel and return to the room to relax and plan my next move. It doesn't take me long to figure out that my best move is to backtrack Karzai from his time in Alameda. I will drive out there to his first known address in this country and snoop around. I check in with Cynthia who is on duty with Gineen. Much to my surprise it is ten o'clock in Boston. I have forgotten the time zone change.

"Cynthia, this is Patrick. Is it too late to talk to Gineen?"

"Yes. She was pooped tonight and went off to sleep about thirty minutes ago."

"Would you tell her that a not-so-secret admirer in California loves her very much and that he will remember about the time zone difference tomorrow?"

"Sure, I'll tell her, like she doesn't know that already. She speaks of you incessantly, to the extent that I am getting tired of you. Aw, just kidding."

"You are forgiven, just this once. Take care."

"You too. Bye now."

I spend some time during this rest of the evening perusing the local newspapers, like the *Examiner*, and then watching or rather trying to watch a movie on TV. I am plainly lonely and miss my honey. I do manage to skim through the papers. All I get from that endeavor is a reminder of how liberal this state is. I mean really. Paying damages to an illegal alien because he was turned over to federal officials for deportation as the law provides? I finally doze off to sleep at midnight after requesting a wake-up call for six a.m. Next morning, I wolf down a quick breakfast and head off for Alameda. I leave early, hoping to find Karzai's former neighbors before they go off to work.

My first stop is his former address. I march up to the door and ring the bell. A somewhat dowdy, middle-aged woman named Amelia opens the door, smiles at me and asks, "Good morning. What can I do for you?"

"I am looking for a gentleman by the name of Karzai."

"I'm sorry but he doesn't live here anymore."

"Perhaps he went back to where he came from. My company owes him some money. Do you know where he came from?"

"Not exactly but it was some foreign country, I believe."

"Like Afghanistan?"

"Yes. That's it."

"It's my understanding that he moved to San Francisco, across the bay."

"Wow that's pretty a pretty expensive place to live. He must have won the lottery."

"I did hear that he came into some money before he left here. His company still has an office here in Alameda. You can try there and see if you can find him."

"Can you tell me where that's located?"

"Not exactly, but it's over in the commercial area closer to the port. It's named Brown and Company. The post office once delivered some of his mail here, so I remember the name but not the address as I told you."

"It shouldn't be difficult to find. You have been very helpful. Thank you so much."

"No problem. Bye now."

Right. Brown and Company. Is he kidding? I stop at the post office and get the address for this company.

"Good morning, my name is Ingel, and I am looking for the address of Brown and Company. My client owes him some money and has been trying unsuccessfully to find him."

"Sure. Here it is right here as he hands me a slip of paper with the address on it."

After thanking him, I find the small office building that

houses Brown and Company. I walk into the lobby and look at the directory. Brown and Company is a trucking company. Interesting, but I need to know more so I take the elevator to the 3rd floor, walk into the office, and march up to the receptionist's desk.

"Hi, my name is Williams," I say. Two can play that phony name game. "I have some bulk chemicals that I need shipped to the east coast."

"Good morning, sir. I'm sorry but the only product we carry are automobiles."

"Interesting. Where do they come from?"

"Mostly from South Korea, the Kia auto company. If there's nothing else, I must go," she says in a rather snippy tone.

You have been more help than you know, I think to myself as I leave the office. A picture is forming in my mind in much the same way a photo would slowly appear as I developed it in a tray in my dark room. Grow the drugs in Afghanistan, trundle it through China to Korea and pack it into new automobiles. Brown and Company then gets to pick off the ones they want. The ones packed with drugs. A very neat and tidy arrangement. Trying to prove this scheme is where the picture gets fuzzy. Very fuzzy. First and foremost, I have no proof of what's going on, so going to the authorities is out. I don't even see any point in informing Allen at this juncture. So, I do what I usually do in this sort of a situation, I eat.

Meanwhile, back at the Brown trucking company, Brown has come back to his office from a business meeting outside of the building. Brown is his real name, not a fake one as I supposed. Meanwhile, unbeknownst to me, Brown is back in his office, having a chat with his secretary. I will find this out at a later date.

"Good morning again, Amelia," he says. "Anything happen while I was out?"

"As a matter of fact, there was. Shortly after you left, a tall handsome guy who said his name was Williams came in and started to ask questions about the company. I cut him off short and he left."

"What did he look like?"

"Well as I said he was tall and good looking with red hair and crystal blue eyes."

"Are you sure he left the building. Could he still be here somewhere?"

"No. Absolutely not. I saw him through the window drive away."

"What was he driving?"

"It looked like a Buick but I'm not certain. Blue for sure. I must tell you that I didn't like him, and I thought he was a lying skunk."

"Would you recognize him if you saw him again?"

"Absolutely, I would."

"Well, be on your toes and let me know immediately if he shows up again. We don't want anyone snooping around here. Our whole operation depends on secrecy. And thank you for being so alert."

"I will let you know if I ever see him again."

While this conversation is going on a few miles away from where I am, I finish my lunch. I have decided to see if I can find some more evidence to support my theory. I am now certain I am correct, but my certainty is useless without some facts. It seems certain that Brown knows which car or cars have the drugs in advance. Probably supplied this information from their Afghani source. It follows that Brown has a record in his office, either on paper or in his computer. I hope not in his computer because I must break into his office and I'm not computer proficient enough to do anything with it. No point waiting any longer, so I'll take my chances tonight. Before that, however, I get on the phone and call Gineen.

"Good evening, sweet love," I greet her. "How are you tonight?"

"I'm doing OK, Patrick. What about you?"

Not wanting to unduly upset her, I respond with "peachy keen."

"Oh sure. How is your investigation going?"

"OK."

"OK. That's it? Come on, Patrick, stop lying to me."

Being evasive has not worked and lying to her is out of the question, so I come clean.

"I've figured most of the scheme out but I'm lacking any factual evidence that I can take to the authorities. The drugs are coming into the port in Kia cars and a company by the name of Brown trucking is distributing them across the country. What remains is for me to obtain some information of the incoming and outgoing vehicles, so I can track the drugs and maybe call in the authorities."

"So, you are going to do what? Break into their office to search for some record?"

"Can't fool you, can I?"

"No and it's time you stopped. I can tell the instant you start being evasive that you are trying to shield me from some bad or dangerous information. You might just as well come right out with it. Save some time. I'm guessing you're going in tonight. Right?"

"Unless I find their security is impenetrable, tonight."

"Just for the record, I'll remind you that you aren't dealing with a nickel and dime operation, so please be wise and careful. I need you back here safe and sound with all of your limbs intact."

"As they say, from your lovely lips to God's ear. Go back to resting and remember I love you very much and that will be the incentive I need to go safely. I love you and good night."

"Good night."

I set my alarm for three o'clock and am in bed by nine. At four in the morning I am at the gate to Brown's office building, having parked my car a block away. I carefully jimmy the lock and slide into the parking lot where I wait for a few minutes. No dogs, no siren, no flood lights, and no watchmen within sight.

Entry into the building is a piece of cake, as is the door to his office. I find nothing on or in his desk that is helpful unless a photograph of a man and a woman can be considered helpful.

Hold on, Miss Snippy Voice is in the photo with her arm around a man's shoulder. That must be Brown himself and if it is, the two are more than friendly. I shine my light around the room and then I spot it. A corkboard full of arrival notices. There is one for today with the destination noted as Chicago, a VIN number, and "blue," noted in a column headed color. I get out quickly and as I do, I see a sign on the door which reads, *Closed for Vacation. See Yard Foreman for Instructions.*

On my way out, I close all the doors carefully and make sure that there are no signs that it has been jimmied. Back to the car to think, in the darkened front seat, staring out at the port facilities, which are now starting to appear in the lightening sky. I wonder if Brown would entrust the delivery of a vast and valuable product to anyone else or if he would do it himself. If it were me, I would do it myself.

I move the car to a location where I can see the front door of Brown's building and wait. An hour or so after sunrise, Brown and Miss Snippy Voice arrive together and enter the building. Their backs are to me, so I can't get a good photo with my Nikon and its long telephoto lens. I sit, slouched down with the camera aimed at the front door. Thirty minutes later the happy pair exit the building providing me with the opportunity for several good shots. I know from the notice on the bulletin board they are headed for Chicago and I have the street address which is on Farwell Avenue. I wait until they are at the Kia and get a shot of them entering it. I quickly leave and drive to the airport in San Francisco, where I book a flight to O'Hare.

I google the Chicago address and find that it is the Rogers Park section just south of the city line with Evanston. No rush since it will take them at least two days to make the trip by car. I have a bite to eat at one of the airport restaurants and eventually board a late flight. It arrives some three hours later, and I reserve a room at an on-site hotel for one night. Dinner and a drink later, I go up to the room and call for a rental car to be reserved for me tomorrow morning. Television for a couple of hours and then off to sleep. A long day. Sleep feels good.

CHAPTER XII

At breakfast the next morning, I realize that I may be getting in over my head. It all started with a simple five-million-dollar theft (if you can consider five million dollars simple) and has now mushroomed into an international drug conglomerate that could be generating hundreds of millions in sales and poisoning millions of young people. I need some help wrestling with my choices for any further action. Therefore, when I finish eating, I call Allen. He picks up on the first ring.

"Good morning, Allen."

"You're up early today. What's going on?'

"Enough so that I need advice on my future direction."

"I am a bottomless pit of advice. Go ahead."

"I flew to San Francisco, you will remember, in search of one individual by the name of Karzai. Well, that eventually led me to a trucking company called Brown and Company. From them I found out that a shipment of Kia automobiles was due in the next day. My gut was telling me that these guys are moving drugs from Afghanistan to the west coast in new cars."

"And you found out about that incoming load of cars, how?"

"Better that you don't know."

"I thought as much."

"Anyhow I took a leap and figured that the drugs were so valuable that Brown would not entrust anyone with their delivery but would do it himself, so I set up nearby his facility and sure enough the next morning he shows up. He and his secretary get in a blue Kia and head east. The fact that the car is blue clinches it in my mind because that color car was highlighted on his arrivals board. I know the destination is in the Rogers Park section of Chicago. Since I know that, I hopped a flight to Chicago and that's where I am now."

"By any chance did you commit any other crimes, other than breaking and entering during your trip? Maybe shoot a security guard or someone else?"

"Not yet but the day is young. I'm glad you have retained your sense of humor. Where do we go from here, Boss?"

"My gut is telling me if we turn over what little evidence we have to the officials, they will likely do nothing about it for lack of useable evidence. And then we settle the claim with Brandt. On the other hand, it's clear to me if the officials will do nothing with what we give them, then we will essentially be complicit in dumping a large load of drugs on this country. What is your good sense telling you?"

"Like you, I doubt that the DEA or the FBI would do anything with what we have. I have only one suggestion. I will continue to do what I was planning on doing. Turn over some more rocks. In other words, keep an eye on Brown's destination until he gets here and see what develops."

"Sounds like an impossible job for one man to do since you don't know when they might show up. Can I get you some help with this surveillance?"

"A good idea. Try to find someone familiar with the area and the retail drug trade if possible."

"I'll call you back within the hour."

Good as his word, he is back forty-five minutes later with a name, George Graf, and a telephone number.

"You can call him right now and he did say he was available right away," Allen explains. "Good luck to the two of you and please take care. No chances please."

"Thanks Allen. Rest assured we will be careful."

"And keep me up to date."

"I will. So long and thanks again."

I hang up on Allen and immediately call the number he gave me for Graf.

"George Graf," he says, "good morning."

"George, Patrick Ingel. I got your name from Timothy Allen back in Boston."

"Yes. He told me you would be calling."

"Listen, it will be a day or two before we have to begin the surveillance Allen called about, but I would like to meet you today and go to the site for a look-see."

"OK. Why don't we meet at the library on Farwell in an hour? I'm driving a yellow Chevy pickup which shouldn't be hard to spot."

"Good. See you in an hour."

He shows up right on the dot. I park and walk over to his truck. Graf gets out and we shake hands and chit chat for a minute of two. Graf is in his 40's, I would say. Tall, thin, with a military style buzz cut.

"Let's take my car, George. It won't stand out like your pickup might."

"Sure. This is my personal vehicle. I use an old Toyota for surveillance jobs."

We drive over to 1433 Farwell, the destination address for Brown, and park at the curb nearby. "C'mon George, let's take a closer look.

We walk on by the place twice and then back to the car, a block away. What we observed is a small ordinary apartment building, a most unlikely place for a major drug operation to be headquartered.

"You know the area, George. What do you think?"

"If I had to guess, I would say that your couple from California will just be picking someone up at that building and going somewhere else to unload their drugs."

"Sounds logical to me. I think we should park my car close enough to the building to photograph or even do a video of them when they arrive. Since I can only guess when they might arrive, let's get here early tomorrow morning and get a parking place close to the building and then just wait. Not very efficient use of our time but it's the only approach I can think of."

"Works for me. I'll bring a deck of cards and whip your ass at gin rummy while we wait. I don't believe I've ever had anyone pay me to play gin rummy before. Bring your wallet and be prepared to lose a bundle. I have a smart phone which we can use for both stills and video."

"A deal. See you here at six tomorrow morning."

"I'll be here."

I get there at five forty-five and have my choice of parking spaces with a good view of the front door. Graf arrives a few minutes later, cruises by in his pickup truck and parks a block away. He walks back to my car and slides into the rear seat where he has a good view of the apartment door and we wait. He has brought his smart phone. He rolls down the window, so he can get some clear photographs, video, and sound if he wants it. We wait and wait. The hours roll by until it is lunch time. Neither of us has brought anything to eat save for a couple of chocolate bars, which don't last long.

At lunchtime, we look at each other and I finally offer, "I couldn't operate your smart phone if my life depended on it. I'll go for food and take a pee, or whatever. I'll take your truck. When I get back you can go."

I find a McDonald's nearby and fill up a bag with hamburgers and fries and head back to the car. I approach it warily but there is nothing wrong.

"Your turn. There's a McDonald's a few blocks away but make sure that you keep your cell phone on, so you can scat back here if they show."

He does. They don't. Hour after hour, we wait. I begin to think about the virtues of gin rummy when suddenly two cars pull up in front of the apartment building. They are identical blue Kias.

"Get busy with your smart phone. They got here just in time. The sun is about to set."

Two people get out of the cars and I can see that they are Brown and his girlfriend. Graf gets a load of photos before the two disappear into the apartment. Thirty minutes later Brown and his girlfriend reappear and get into their car while a third guy comes out of the apartment and gets into the second one. Both cars take off and we follow.

"I hope you got some good shots of that third guy."

"I dunno. There's not too much light left. I think we'll have something useful. Least I hope so."

I begin to see the last part of their plan. The guys in the first KIA will deliver it to its proper location, a Kia dealer, no doubt. The second one driven by Brown is the one packed with drugs and will land somewhere in the area where the drugs can be unpacked and probably repackaged in street-level packages for sale locally. Pretty neat. They have both the wholesale end and the retail end. How do I know this? I don't for sure but again, my instincts have been good so far.

"We're going to follow Brown and take a chance that he doesn't spot us."

I keep well back from him, and he eventually turns into a narrow, one-way alley-like street and then into a small garage in the middle of the block. I drive slowly by and make a mental note of the street number even though I don't know the name of the street.

"You know where we are, Graf?"

"Yeah, I do."

"Then I guess we know where the center of their drug operation is."

"Come on. You don't know anything of the sort. They may have simply garaged their vehicle for the night."

"Damn this case. I'm getting sick and tired of it," I say. "Let's circle the block and park where we have a view of that garage."

We do that. I find a curb space where we can sit and wait. Something I've had enough of. Nevertheless, we are still waiting an hour later when my cell rings. It is Allen.

"Patrick, we have a rather startling development in the case which seems to get more complex by the day."

"And we have a small development here. We have followed Brown's Kia to a small garage here in Chicago, not too far from the apartment building."

"I think I am going to have to pull you off the drug chase

for a while and have you fly back to Boston immediately. Our man Ponce has turned up dead in the woods out west of here and it certainly looks like murder at this point."

"Strange, indeed. Do you want me to call Graf off the job or leave him here to see if he can learn anything?"

"Hard for me to make a decision from here. Use your best judgement about that."

"OK. By the time I get to O'Hare and book a seat back to Boston, it may be too late to get out tonight, but I will try."

"Just do the best you can."

"Sure. Later."

Graf has been following the conversation and obviously knows there is a major development. "What's up? Are you calling me off the job?"

'It depends. I am being pulled back to Boston where this complex case has just gotten even more bizarre. If you think you can wait out Brown and confirm what we suspect, namely that this place is the key processing center for the drugs, then stay on the job for as long as you can hold out. If the answer to that is yes, I will wait while you get some food and take a pee break."

"I'll try, at least for another six hours or so. Thanks for waiting. I'll be back in fifteen minutes or so."

"Go."

Graf is back quickly with a bag full of sandwiches, donuts, and coffee.

"Looks like enough for a week. Here's my cell phone number. Call me if you learn anything that confirms what we both know. Remember that pictures and videos will be very helpful. I'm out of here. See you later."

"You take care and have a good flight."

149

As I expected, there are no seats available back to Boston tonight. I reserve a seat on an early morning flight and then head for an airport hotel. I set an alarm for five a.m. and fall quickly asleep. I have time in the morning for a quick breakfast at the hotel, drop off my rental car, and get to the terminal in time to make my flight. I call Sam and ask him to pick me up at Logan. The flight home is uneventful. The kind I prefer. Sam and I am home by eleven. I am met by Cynthia, who is startled when I step through the door.

"Hey," she says. "I thought you were on the west coast or some other exotic place."

"I was but I had to come back sooner than I thought because of some developments. Where's Gineen?"

"She's upstairs resting. Bad night and morning with some nasty nausea symptoms."

"I'm going up to say hello."

"OK, but if she's sleeping try not to wake her. She needs the sleep more than she needs anything right now."

I tip toe up the stairs and into the bedroom. She is sound asleep. I quietly gather up some fresh clothes and am about to slip out the door when she wakes up.

"Hey, who's that sneaking around my bedroom? I'm calling the cops."

"I deserve to go to jail for waking you up? You are a sight for sore eyes, lovely lady."

"Such bullshit. I'm a mess and you know it."

"You do look a bit pale."

"Thanks, but I know exactly how I look. We have a mirror in the bathroom, y'know."

I lean over and kiss her forehead which is very warm.

"What's with the clothes and suitcase? I look so bad, you

are leaving me? Hellava husband you are. I want a divorce."

"Sure, no problem. Have your lawyer call my lawyer. All I want is this condo. You can have everything else."

"Funny, Mr. Numb Nuts, that's the only thing we have. Call off the divorce. Hon, what are you doing here?"

"The good news is I am finished with California and Chicago. The bad news is our security guard, Ponce, has been found murdered somewhere in the western part of the state and I'm on my way there to see what I can find out."

"Well go then. By the time you get back I probably will have stopped vomiting and we can go out for a great Italian dinner at your favorite restaurant."

I lean over her and kiss both cheeks and her forehead. "It's a date. Good night."

"Bye."

I call Allen to get directions. He lets me know that Ponce's body was found in the Lawrence Swamp. It's located in the western part of the state beyond the Quabbin Reservoir, the major source of water for the Boston area.

"I'm not sure what town that's in and who has jurisdiction," Allen admits, "but I think it's Amherst."

"OK. I'm on my way. Call you later."

CHAPTER XIII

Amherst, the site of one location of the University of Massachusetts, is a two and a half hour drive. When I get there, I head straight for the police station. I am referred to a Detective Kennedy.

"Good morning, detective," I say as I enter this office. "My name is Patrick Ingel. I'm a private investigator from Boston. I'm working on a large case of theft. A man by the name of Ponce was a suspect. I understand that he has been murdered out here. Seems like a long way to go to kill someone."

"No, he wasn't killed in the swamp. No sign of blood around the body. So, he was killed somewhere else and brought here and buried in a shallow grave. The location was just off Well 4 Road. The area is the location of a well that supplies the town with water. Only one way in and one way out. Very remote. Hardly any traffic, vehicular or pedestrian. We probably would never have found the grave, were it not for a couple of teenagers with a dog. The dog found the body. Sniffed it out and dug it up. I don't know a better location to bury a murder victim. That suggests the perp was someone who was familiar with the area. Don't you agree?"

"I do. But the Ponce lived outside of Boston. Hard to imagine that someone from around here drove there, killed him and then brought him back here."

"I wasn't suggesting that at all. Simply that the perp knew

the swamp and how remote it is."

"I get it," I say, catching onto his suspicions. "How was he killed?"

"Single shot to the heart. Don't know any more than that. The state police now have the case and they will get an autopsy done and go from there. They might appreciate hearing from you. At this point they don't know much about him. You could probably help them out."

"Give me a name and number and I will get in touch with them."

"Sure. It's Detective Carrington at the North Hampton Barracks, B6."

He gives me the number and I call as I head for the car.

"May I speak to Detective Carrington, please? My name is Patrick Ingel and I am a private investigator from Boston."

"May I tell him what it's about?"

"Yes. I am working on a large theft case and have some information about the body found in the Laurence Swamp."

"I'm sure he will want to talk to you. Hold on while I track him down."

I hear the line beep. The line rings and rings until another voice answers.

"Hello, this is Jim Carrington. I understand that you have some information on the body that was recently found in Amherst."

"I do, and I think it might make your investigation go a bit faster."

"We could use some help on that one. Are you in Boston?"

"No. I have just talked to the Amherst P.D. and I'm available to talk with you right now."

"Good. Ask for me when you get here."

It's a quick trip over to the barracks and I get there in twenty minutes including a drive through a McDonald's to get a hamburger and fries to munch on while I drive.

I am greeted by a lovely dispatcher when I arrive. She walks me back to Carrington's office where we introduce ourselves and sit down to talk. Carrington makes some notes while we go over what I know.

"Detective, let me start at the beginning. I am working on a theft of about five million dollars' worth of artwork. My client is Tim Allen, whose American Independence Insurance Company insured the artwork. I'll give you his number and you can verify what I tell you. To make a long story short, the security guard at the mansion of the owner of the art is named Elvin Ponce and he was on duty at the time of the theft. Doing some back tracking on him I discovered that he was probably involved in a similar case in Chicago. There appears, almost certainly, to be a connection with a large importer of illegal drugs. If you like, I can look at the body to see if I can ID him, for what that's worth."

"That would obviously speed up our work. The medical examiner has scheduled a postmortem for tomorrow. I'd be delighted if you could drive over to the morgue with me and see if you can ID him."

"Be happy to do that and that might speed up my investigation as well, providing I can confirm my suspicions."

"Why don't you leave your car here and drive over to the mortuary with me?"

"OK."

At the mortuary, the attendant pulls out a box and uncovers the face. It's Elvin Ponce.

"That's him," I say confidently. "No question about it.

That's Elvin Ponce. Will you be taking fingerprints from him?"

"Yes, we will, and we will look at state and federal databases looking for a match. I'll keep you informed on that. Let's get back to your car so you get on your way home."

"Sounds good to me after traipsing all over the country for what seems like a month."

"I'd like to thank you so much for being straight with us," Carrington says. "You have really accelerated the state's investigation tremendously."

"Well that works both ways and I thank you for your help as well."

"You take care. If my work on this case takes me to Boston, I will certainly give you a call and maybe we can get together to compare notes."

"Absolutely. Be sure to call."

I have the urge to try out my rental car on the Mass Turnpike to see where it will top-out. I control that urge and stay at ten miles above the limit. That gets me back home right at dinnertime. I walk in just as Franny, Cynthia, and Gineen are sitting down to dinner.

"What a lucky guy I am to have three lovely women to share dinner with. Gineen, you look terrific. Your color is great, and I can see the sparkle in your eye."

I hug and kiss her longingly and whisper in her ear. "I love you. How about dinner out, a movie, and then making love until three in the morning?"

"Get hold of yourself, detective. That would be rushing things. I am so much better but easy does it. I do have some very good news. It's likely that I am done with the chemo, but I won't know for sure until my doctor's appointment tomorrow morning."

"I can't think of any better news unless it were that you were pregnant."

"Oh, eat your dinner and stop rushing things. Have some tofu."

This brings snickers from the nurses, but I surprise them by taking a heaping plateful. Ugh! It's awful but I work my way through it.

The phone interrupts my eating just then.

"Hello, Patrick Ingel, world's best detective."

"Really? I thought Sherlock Holmes held that title. Knock it off, Graf. You are interrupting my first meal in ages with my wife. What's up?"

"It looks like we have confirmed that the garage on Farwell is the distribution center. Brown and his girl left the place a few minutes ago in a taxi, leaving the Kia inside."

"Good. Did you get photos?"

"Indeed, I did. Stills and videos. All good quality."

"Make some copies for your files and send the originals to me. Good job. There will be a handsome bonus in it for you."

"No need, just doin' my job."

"Really? Shall I give it to my favorite charity?"

"Aw, OK, I'll spare you the trouble of doing that. I'll take it for my own personal charity."

"Got a pen handy? Take down my mailing address. I'll look forward to receiving those photos in a few days."

"Thanks again and have a good evening,"

I just get started on my tofu when I am saved by the bell again.

"Hello. Patrick Ingel. Allen here. Bring me up to date."

"What? No good evening?"

"No, how are you feeling after your arduous trip?"

"Tim, I am having the very first dinner with my wife in days and days. How about I call you back at eight?"

"Sure."

No excuse this time and I tear into my tofu while Gineen watches with a bit of a smirk on her beautiful face.

"We can get you a rib eye steak if you want. I know you hate that stuff."

"It's OK. If you can eat this stuff, so can I. Maybe I'll end up looking as good as you do."

"Oh nonsense, I'm going to cook you up steak and put you out of your rather obvious misery. French fries?"

Real food. I don't argue the point. Besides it's so good seeing her busy in the kitchen and enjoying it.

I scarf down my meal and then pick up my giggling wife and carry her up the stairs to the bedroom.

We are lying in each other's arm an hour later and I whisper in her ear, just before we slip off to sleep, "This is one of the best nights in my life."

"Don't rush things, I haven't been checked out at Dana Faber yet."

"I know but that's just a formality and tomorrow we will know for sure," I say. "Good night, love."

"Good night. You are the best."

I decide not to argue with that even though I know I am next to the best. Just as I was dropping off, I remember that I had forgotten to call Allen. So, I get fired. Doesn't matter. I have my healthy wife back and that is more important than anything. At breakfast the next morning, I tell Gineen about forgetting the call to Allen.

"Oh, my God, I distracted you from your work and now I

feel so guilty."

"Knock it off. My work means nothing to me. The future hasn't looked this bright since we left the Casino."

"C'mon Patrick. You have a commitment. Get the hell on the telephone and call him right now, before I punch you out."

"Now, I know you're better. Been a while since I heard those fighting words. OK, I'll do my duty and call him."

Allen picks up on the first ring. "Tim Allen."

"Allen, this is Patrick. I owe you an apology. I totally forgot to call you last night. I was preoccupied with Gineen."

"No apology necessary. Does this mean she's worse?"

"No, just the opposite. She's recovering nicely. We have an appointment at Dana Farber this morning to see what they say. I'm guessing that they will find no trace of the cancer and dismiss us."

"I didn't know you had a medical degree, but I will second the motion. Please give me a call this afternoon and we'll arrange a time when we can sit down and sort through where we are and where we go from here. Later."

With that, I hang up and I head for the car.

"Hey man," Gineen says, stopping me at the door. "Where are you going."

"To get the car," I say.

"We're walking. Think you can make the three blocks."

I sigh. "Walk it is."

There is a lightness to her gait that tells me that this ordeal is done. At Dana Faber, her doctor probes, fondles, and then takes some more x-rays. When he's done, he invites us into his office for a chat.

"Gineen, I have good news for you. As far as we can tell

there is absolutely no sign of any cancer cells left in your breasts or any other organ in your body."

Tears well up in her eyes. "Oh, I can't tell you how happy I am to hear you say that. Does that mean I am totally discharged from your care and there will be no more chemotherapy?"

"Yes, with one proviso. I will ask you to keep your eye on things. If any unusual symptoms pop up anywhere in your body, I want to hear from you immediately. And if nothing does show up, I expect to see you here annually for a checkup."

With that, he stands and extends his hand, but she will have none of that. She brushes his hand aside and grabs him in an emotional hug with tears running down her cheeks, all the while laughing with happiness. My own eyes tear up a bit, but I resist the urge to hug and kiss him. Gineen literally dances down the street all the way to the condo, causing a few bewildered looks from drivers and pedestrians. No sooner than I have closed the door then she jumps on me and wraps her legs around my waist and her arms around my shoulders, nearly knocking me over.

CHAPTER IV

"We don't have time to go upstairs, love me on the sofa. Right this instant."

I follow her orders and then we make it upstairs later for a quieter session.

"Oh Patrick, I can't tell you how good I feel." And then the weeping starts all over again. "Sorry, but these are happy tears. I hope you just made me pregnant with triplets.

"Hey, be careful what you wish for. Neither of us could handle triplets now, not even twins."

"OK, I'll settle for one. But don't think for a minute that I will stop there. I won't raise an only child."

"Sure. We will raise a family – a girl for you, a boy for me, ta da, da."

"Really nice voice, old man, but don't give up the day job just yet. Now lunch, a pregnant woman needs her vitamins and absolutely no more alcohol."

"Not even a bottle of champagne to celebrate?"

"Well, maybe one."

"Don't you think you should wait for a doctor to tell you that you are pregnant?"

"Not necessary, I tell you. I know for sure."

"Well, let me do the honor and make lunch. Tofu for you and a small steak for me. After all a working detective needs to keep up his strength."

We have a quick lunch. Food doesn't seem to be on either of our minds, even after all that exercise.

"Why don't you call Cynthia and Franny and tell them the good news and then I will call Allen and set up a meeting for this afternoon."

In a few minutes, the two nurses come in, all excited, acting more like old friends than caretakers.

Gineen says to me, "You will remember that I promised to buy Sam and his wife dinner as soon as I was over the treatment and I intend to do that now. Is tomorrow night OK with you?"

"Probably, but I'll know better after my meeting with Allen this afternoon. Right now, I don't know what our plan of action will be and where it might take me."

I meet with Allen at Jake Wirth's and I bring him up to date.

"Let me backtrack to the beginning," I say. "At this point I am certain I know the roadmap of how the drugs are coming into this country. They are shipped from Afghanistan to Mr. Karzai in San Francisco in Kia automobiles. The cars are routed to various parts of the country by one Brown and Company. The drugs, however, all go to a central place in Chicago where they are processed for retail sales. Your man Graf has managed to capture Brown and his secretary entering a garage-like building on his smart phone. He has both stills and a video. They are very clever about this and leave the processing plant in an identical blue Kia. Presumably they drive that one to the proper dealer. I didn't have him follow them, but the end location is probably close by. As you know a body was recently found in a remote place in central Massachusetts called the Laurence Swamp.

The Swamp is in the town of Amherst. I went there at your direction and positively identified the body as Ponce for the local and then the state police who have taken over the case. It's clearly a murder case. He was killed by a single bullet to the head from a small caliber pistol from close range. You could speculate that he knew the killer because powder burns on his face indicate the shooter was very close to him. This is, of course a bit of speculation on my part but the police seemed to agree with this. He was buried in a shallow grave in the woods not far off the road. The body might never have been found without the help of a young couple hiking with their dog. Since the body was freshly buried, it's safe to conclude the killing took place within a few days of when it was found. He was shot elsewhere as confirmed by the lack of blood in and around the scene. Although I was only there for a few hours, I did develop a rapport with both police departments. The State Police Detective Wilson will be coming to talk to us, and I feel sure that he will clue us in on the results of the post and his lab's forensic examination. One thing both investigators agree on is that the perp was familiar with the swamp location and could not have picked it by chance. In this computer age, I don't think that is automatically true. But maybe."

"Patrick, what are your guts telling you about how and why this happened?"

"The temptation is to dump this on Brandt's head and that may or may not be the case. I doubt that Brandt would dirty his own hands with this killing, but he could have used Swazey or some other hired hand to do the job. If it was someone else, he would be a loose end and he would be wise to get as far away and as fast as he can from Brandt and

Swazey. As far as motive goes, it would be easy to theorize that Ponce tried to use his knowledge of the theft of the art to wrangle a larger share, maybe all of it. Possibly they were just getting rid of a loose end, or a weak link. The police have treated the story low key with the local papers. They have not publicly identified Ponce, but the medical examiner has scheduled a postmortem, so they can't keep it secret for very much longer. At least for the present time the killer might very well think the body has not been found. The state police lab is combing Ponce's clothing and the gravesite for any additional evidence. You are up to date now except for one piece of good news. Gineen has been given a clean bill of health from her doctors. I have to tell you that is one big load off both our minds."

"Ah. Congratulations. That is the best news. As far as the case goes, I think it would be prudent not to take any overt action before we consult with Wilson. However, that doesn't mean you should stop thinking about investigative steps we could take with their cooperation."

"I won't. In fact, I have some ideas percolating in my head already. Of course, I gave Wilson your name and number and he will be in touch within a few days. Let me know when he calls."

"I certainly will. Give my regards to Gineen, please."

"Absolutely."

When I arrive back at the condo Gineen is busily engaged in cleaning the condo.

"Woman," I say as I walk into the condo, "you are making me look bad as a housekeeper."

"Not hard to do. It was really messy. How did your meeting with Allen go?"

"After bringing him up to date, we decided against any overt action until the state police are in touch, which I think will be within a few days. He sent his regards by the way and he seemed genuine about that."

"Thank him for me next time you see him,"

"I will. Any luck with Sam?"

"Oh yes. They are coming over tonight. I thought the Cask 'N Flagon would work well, so I made reservations. OK with you?"

"Why not. The Red Sox are out of town. We might even find a parking place."

"I told them to dress casually, so you too."

"There's another way? I'm going to take a shower, Care to join me?"

"After doing all this cleaning, you bet I do."

You could say that we both clean up nicely. Sam and his wife Nancy show up at five and we drive them to the restaurant. Sam shows me where to park. His wife is a bit on the frumpy side but proves to be very good company – funny and irreverent. They both are excellent company and we have a great time. Gineen outdoes herself with a bottle of champagne. We toast to health and happiness.

"You two have any children?" Gineen asks Nancy.

"Yes ma'am," she responds and sips her champagne, "we have two – a six-year-old son and a nine-year-old daughter. They are a handful, but we have a great time together. Now that they are both in school, it gives me time to think about going back to work part time."

"I envy you," Gineen says and touches my arm. "Patrick and I will be having our first not very long from now."

On the way out, Nancy turns to Gineen and says, "The

next time you will come to our house."

"Great. I would love to meet your kids. We'll do it soon. Good night."

"Good night and thank you so much for a good time."

Closing the door, I say, "I don't know about you, but I am in the best frame of mind. Let's go to bed."

"I accept your invitation, but I have to warn you, I seem to have misplaced my pjs."

"Knock it off, Gineen. Just sleep tonight."

"Oh, you, big baby. Alright you are off the hook. Tomorrow is another day."

I sleep on my back with my arm under her neck and her fragrant hair all over my shoulder and chest. We are both refreshed by a good night's sleep and after breakfast I go into the office to noodle a bit about the case.

"Oh, Patrick, I forgot to tell you. Yesterday I talked to Sally. She and Roger are coming for a visit. We are going to have such a good time."

"Indeed, we will. It will be nice to see them. Did she say anything about marriage?"

"Nope, not a peep. Wouldn't it be great if they tied the knot up here?"

"Well, it would be nice, but I think they would prefer to do that in their hometown in Connecticut where most of their relatives and friends live. After all, we were married there ourselves."

"You're probably right."

"When are they getting here?"

"Sally said in a couple of days. But she didn't give me anything more specific than that."

"I'm going into our office to do some thinking about my

case. You?"

"Too beautiful to stay indoors all day. I'm going out for a walk. Maybe up to Coolidge Corner, maybe down the Emerald Necklace. So good to be *free* again. I'll see you later. Old stick in the mud workaholic."

A hug and a peck on the cheek and she's out the door bursting with energy and vitality. I promised Allen that I would wait for Wilson to get here before I took any overt action to solve the case. What the hell? A little snooping around isn't overt action. So, I leave Gineen a note to let her know that I will be back for lunch, suggesting a deli lunch in Coolidge Corner. I drive out to the Brandt Mansion and park where I have a view of the gate to the mansion. Everything looks normal as far as I can see. It's an hour before anything at all happens. At that point, a Mercedes sedan arrives, and a new security guard opens the gate. The driver gets out of the car and the two have a short conversation. The driver points to a large dent in the otherwise pristine vehicle. When they finish, he gets back into the car and drives up to the mansion, disappearing inside. I get a few good shots of the two of them with my telephoto lens. I drive off a few minutes later and return to a different parking spot on the same side of the street as the guard station, a bit farther away. I hope he has not noticed me before and will not now. Nothing stirs for the next hour and I figure I have exhausted my supply of luck and drive away. Back home to the condo.

"Hey detective, where have you been?" Gineen greets me as I walk through the door. "I thought you would be waiting for me in your office."

"Well I decided to take a drive out to the Brandt mansion and look around a bit."

"Wait a minute I could swear I heard you say that Allen didn't want you to take any overt action until Wilson got here and you worked out a plan together."

"Aw. I just sat in my car for a few hours and snapped a few pictures. I wouldn't call that overt."

"Well I would. And so would Webster. Means done in the open dummy!"

"Nah, I was hidden in the car."

"You are impossible sometimes and this is one of them. You have no idea what those guys are up to except they have a zillion dollar drug empire and have likely murdered someone recently. If the cops drag you home in a box one day, I am going to be damn pissed off at you."

"Relax. Look, no broken bones, gunshot wounds or even a minor bruise."

"You are exasperating sometimes," she says. "This is no way for a newly minted father to act."

With that she winds up and whacks me in the stomach.

"Ow. And that's no way for a maybe mother to act. I'm not sure I can eat anything after that punch but let's walk over to Zaftig's Deli and I'll try." Good to see that she is all the way back to fighting shape. Secretly I am happy about that, but I can't let her know that and open myself up for more punishment.

"Oh bull. If you were on the Titanic as it was sinking, you would be gobbling down a steak and French fries."

We walk the short distance to the deli, and I manage to down a fat pastrami sandwich, potato salad, and coleslaw.

"You need some exercise after that meal fat boy! C'mon, I'll race you home."

No contest. She is sitting on the front step waiting for me

when I pull up, huffing and puffing.

"I'm putting you on an exercise routine starting today. I'll have you in shape in two to three weeks. Get inside and I'll outline it for you."

"Y'know that gives me an idea. Since you are so daffy about exercise, why don't you open a studio and make some money. You really do need to get back to work as much as I need exercise."

"Not a good time for a pregnant woman to start such a business."

"Oh Gineen, you don't know if you are pregnant and even if you are, you can train someone else to take over."

"Never mind that for a few minutes. C'mon inside and let me outline a program for you."

Once we're inside, she stands in front of me and begins outlining her plan. "Sit down there and listen. First thing in the morning, you do set of muscle stretches while laying on your back. Then a series sitting on a chair, mostly muscle stretching. After then a series standing up, mostly muscle strengthening, including touching your toes thirty times and then at least thirty pushups. Follow this later in the day with some running, starting small and working up to at least four miles."

"I see and about how long does this take?"

"About two to three hours."

"Yikes. Doesn't leave much time to eat, let alone work."

"You eat too much. If you are willing to try them, I will show you each exercise and get you to do them correctly. You game?"

"I suppose so. What have I to lose?"

"A few pounds of flab, maybe."

We spend another hour with Gineen demonstrating each exercise and waiting patiently while I get it right.

"Now, starting tomorrow morning, you do all of the exercises except the running before you have breakfast."

"Hey, that means getting up several hours earlier in the morning if I'm to stay on a normal work schedule, which I must."

"Well worth the sacrifice, I'd say."

"There goes my cell. Don't go away, woman." I answer the call. "Hello, Ingel, here."

"Allen on this end. I have just heard from Wilson and he wants to meet with us tomorrow morning at nine. He's staying at the Parker House and I told him we'd come over there for breakfast. OK with you?"

"Fine. See you there." I hang up and return to Gineen. "Back to work tomorrow morning, Gineen. I'm meeting Allen and Wilson at the Parker House for breakfast."

"Good. You've had enough of a vacation. Let's watch a movie tonight. The other night, Nancy told me about one called *A Dog of Flanders*."

"Umm, sounds like a kid's picture to me."

"She assured me it wasn't. Anyhow, we can try it out and if we don't like it, we'll find something else."

After a delicious Italian meal by an Irish lass, we sit back and watch the movie. We watch all of it because it's just so charming. Nancy was right. There is a dog in the picture but it's not a kid's picture. It's mostly about art and following your talents, no matter how old you are.

CHAPTER XV

I'm up at four the next morning to allow time for the exercise routine. It goes well but does take me almost two hours. I shave and shower, eat breakfast and then hop the Huntington Ave Trolley downtown and walk the rest of the way to the Parker House, where Allen and Wilson are waiting for me.

"Good morning, gentlemen. Sorry I'm late but my wife started me on an exercise routine which took me almost two hours this morning."

"You should get rid of that woman," says Wilson as he thrusts out his hand. He could stand to lose fifty pounds, so I suppose exercise to him means winding his watch.

We eat breakfast and talk small talk as we linger over second cups of coffee.

"Patrick, I see a twinkle in your eye so why don't you go first. I know that you have been thinking about ways to solve the theft portion of this thing which has mushroomed into an international conspiracy."

"I have done some thinking and the other day I spent some time observing the Brandt mansion. Not much happened there except I got a photo of his new security guard and the only other person to show up. He was driving a Mercedes sedan. He and the guard had a brief conversation, from what I could tell, about large dents in the front quarter panel and the driver's door. I only spent a few hours there and nothing else happened, so I left. I was especially careful to park in places where I was inconspicuous."

"I hope so because we didn't want them forewarned, Patrick."

Allen is clearly pissed at me, and in retrospect, I am sorry. I took that chance, even though I was confident that I was not observed.

"Why don't you get the photos to Wilson, so he can try to match the photos with names and addresses. Did you manage to get the license plate number of the car?"

"Well it shows up in the photo but it's near the periphery and not clearly legible."

"Let's have a look. I don't recognize either bloke, but we'll search our file in the state and forward a copy to the FBI. They have better technology than we do as well has a much bigger data base. I'm glad we have these photos because it gives us a powerful place to start. Thanks for the good work."

I can feel Allen relax and any thoughts he might have had about rebuking me for violating his dictum are gone.

"The medical examiner has completed his postmortem examination of Ponce. While it is not yet filed, he did give me a chance to look it over. He has confirmed what we already pretty much knew – that the decedent was not killed in the swamp but somewhere else and dumped there. Also, he was able to approximate the time of death but not at all precisely. His conclusion on that is within two to three days before we found him. We had Ponce's fingerprints on file because of his security guard job. We will give those to the FBI to search for any other matches in their files. That work will take as much as four days due to their heavy workload."

Allen interrupts with the following comment, "Perhaps I

can try to speed that up with a telephone call."

"Good luck with that," Wilson says. "Our tech guys have a bunch of fiber and soil evidence, but, of course, nothing to match it with, yet."

"Well I do know the FBI director fairly well. Let me give him a call right now."

Allen whips out his cell and dials a number he knows by heart. I guess he really does know the director *really* well.

"Good morning. This is Tim Allen of American Independence Insurance. Could I please speak to Director Pritchard, if he's in? No, he won't know. This is an entirely new matter that I could use a little help with. Sure, I'll wait."

A few minutes later he resumes the conversation with, "Good morning, Dale. I need a bit of a favor from you. The company has a five million dollar claim we are working on. In the process of working on it, we have uncovered a worldwide drug empire and finally a murder, as well. Your agency has taken over the case, but the processing of some fingerprints is slowing us down at this point. It would be helpful if you could speed this up a bit. No, that's all I need. I know it's not much, but timing is critical to us at this point. That would be great. See you and Kathleen for dinner next trip to the District of Confusion." With that he pockets the cell. "Gentlemen, we'll have our fingerprint info by the end of the day."

I don't know about the others, but I am impressed by this unassuming gentleman who I am working for.

"Now with that out of the way, let's work out a rough program to bring these cases to successful conclusions."

He has quietly taken over the leadership of the group.

"What we find out from the fingerprint information may

very well alter our course, but it will be helpful to have a rough structure, so we know where we want to go," Allen says. "Now, we essentially have three cases. One is the original theft of the art works that Patrick is working on for me. Second is shutting down the drug ring and third is the murder of Ponce. They may or may not be related but my guts are telling me that if we solve one of them, we will likely have gone a long way to the other two. By the way, does anyone have a problem bringing the DEA into the drug case? To me it seems logical to do that because of their experience. Patrick, do you have any thoughts on the art theft case?"

"Tim, in the bottom of my gut is a very strong feeling that all these cases are related to each other and they revolve around our client Brandt and his crew. With that said, they are my number one suspects but as of this time, I have absolutely no evidence to prove that. I suppose the next step for me would be to get into the mansion and look for the art or a clue to where it is. I don't believe he would be stupid to keep it there. But I can't get in there without a search warrant. If we were successful in getting a judge to grant a warrant, which I doubt, and didn't find anything then we have alerted the thief and it would accomplish nothing but to drive him deeper underground. If the FBI and police were not here I would suggest to my client that I go into the mansion in the middle of the night and look for the art or a clue to its whereabouts."

Eyes open wide and Allen gasps, and I sit down. There is silence in the room. I believe they are both waiting for someone to speak and they would love to send me in there in the middle of the night. I break the silence with, "Just my dark side showing, guys."

Breaking the silence, Wilson offers the following, which I fully expected, "We are officers of the law and cannot condone nor overlook illegal tactics." A small, barely detectable smile forms at the corners of his mouth. It's a message to me, no doubt about it. They will look the other way and disown me should I go in and get caught. That's exactly what I would do if I was a lawman in this predicament.

"Gentlemen, I suggest that we break up this love fest and reconvene later in the day when we get our fingerprint data."

Everyone shakes their head in the affirmative and we leave after Allen picks up the check. He tugs my sleeve on the way out the door.

"Come on, Patrick, and I'll drive you to Brookline, so we can talk some more privately."

"Sure."

"You are not going to like what I am going to tell you."

"Aw, Tim, I already know. You have gone way out on a limb and you will totally disavow me like the others will if I get caught."

"You know I would not want to do that. However, I would have no other choice. I would, of course, soften the tone of what I would say and refer to your prior good work, but disown you I would, in no uncertain terms."

"There is one thing you could do to help."

"What's that?"

"Simply call Brandt in the early evening and let me know if he's in the mansion or not."

"I can do that."

"Thanks."

He leaves me at the condo after chatting briefly with Gineen.

"Gineen, I've got to go shopping for a few clothes this afternoon," I say. "It won't be long."

"Clothes. What clothes? You have more clothes than I do."

"I need a pair of black dungarees and a black windbreaker."

"What in the world for?"

"I can't lie to you, honey bunny, I am going to do something a bit dangerous tonight."

"Don't give me that honey bunny crap. What is it?"

"I'm going to go into the Brandt mansion tonight to look for some answers to this case. If I get caught, everyone, including Tim will be disowning me, and I would likely end up in jail for a while."

"You're joking right. You'll be in jail while I have our first baby? Are you nuts? Or just crazy? You told me once that no job is worth more to you than I am. Did you not?" Her voice is rising to a pitch that tells me I need to find a way to calm her down.

"Look, Gineen. Calm down. I promise that I won't do anything until we have talked it all out and then if you say no go, it's no go. OK?"

"You won't be able to charm me into letting you perform this nutty stunt, Patrick. So, don't even think about trying to."

"This charming guy wouldn't think about charming you. I know better. I think I need a drink to give us time to sort this all out and calm me down. You?"

"A double Bushmills, straight up."

"Oh boy, you must really be upset. I apologize for having done that, but you asked, and I wouldn't lie to you ever. You must know that."

"Of course, I do, and I'm sorry I got so emotional. It's

just that I can't stand the idea of you getting hurt doing something like this. It's not the possible jail time I'm worried about at all. Brandt and his minions have so much to lose and if they catch you, there is no question you will end up in a grave somewhere deep in the Maine woods."

"Gineen, I fully understand your fears. I doubt there is much chance that Brandt's crew would do anything more than call the cops. The cops already know that I am going to try this and if I should disappear, that would be the end of Brandt. You once said that you wouldn't want to stand in the way of my work. I'm a detective and I take risks, all the way back to my work in New Haven and certainly at the Casino Royale as you know. If I go in and find the evidence I want, it will blow up this drug ring and save lots of young kids from getting hooked and worse."

This is the thought that finally brings her back from the brink. I see her give me a slight but knowing head shake in the affirmative.

"Oh, Patrick, I won't stand in your way on this as long as you promise that you won't take any unnecessary risks. Please forgive me for being so emotional," she says as the tears start again.

"Now come with me upstairs. No drinks, no dinner, just love."

Love this time means holding each other in silence for an hour. After that I go out to a local clothing store and get the black clothes that I need. When I return to the condo, she has dinner prepared, complete with candlelight and champagne. Using my good sense, I defer from making a bad joke about the last supper.

At eight Allen calls and says, "He's in for the night."

At nine, I go to bed on the downstairs couch which causes Gineen to ask, "I thought you were going out tonight to break and enter."

"I am, but I will wait to three a.m. or so to go in."

"You want me to come along. I always wanted to drive a get-away car?"

"Good to see that your sense of humor is back. Go on to bed and I'll see you for breakfast."

"Breakfast, Sherlock. Please be careful."

"I will, love."

I set the alarm for two a.m. and fall asleep within a few minutes.

At two a.m., I get dressed in my black t-shirt, black jeans, and black windbreaker and head out for the mansion. My first inclination is to take my .38 revolver and tuck it into my jeans, covering it with the windbreaker. Nah. Breaking and entering is bad enough, but doing it armed is decidedly worse.

The trip out to Lincoln is fast with very little traffic on the roads at that hour. I drive slowly past the gate and the guardhouse and park well beyond it around a curve in the road. There was a light on in the guard house, but I could not tell if it was manned. What would be the point in having it empty during the night when most crimes are committed?

With the help of a stepladder that I brought, I get over the fence easily. I sit motionless with my back to the fence for five minutes. Nothing is moving. No guard dogs, thankfully. The mansion is dark, save for a few lighted windows on the third level which I know are the servants' quarters. I stand and move very slowly, a step at a time to the back of the building. It's my intention to enter from the patio, which, like most patios, has sliding glass doors. From past visits, I know that inside the doors is a dining room and a kitchen. After standing still for another five minutes, I jimmy the doors as I have many times in the past. I slide them open a bit and wait to see if any alarms go off. They don't.

I know that Brandt's office, which is my goal, is on the far end of the building. Using a tiny penlight, I slowly make my way toward it. Before I get there, I am startled by a light that goes on in the kitchen. I duck into a closet and wait. Someone is in the kitchen making coffee or tea. I wait until the light goes off and I can hear someone making their way to the stairs. It's getting late and I worry about people getting up early, so I start out for the office. Wait a minute, it might be useful to look at the clothes in the closet which are mostly outdoor jackets.

I slide back in and use my light to pick out one which is obviously a man's. I slip it on and head for the office. It is full of file cabinets and desks. There are several computers which I would like to carry away with me, but they will be missed, tipping Brandt off that someone has been in the house. I find nothing at all and am about to leave empty handed when I notice a note pad next to a telephone. On the top sheet is the word "Amherst" and a number. Bingo! I memorize the number and make my way back toward the patio door. I squeeze out the door and manage to latch it. Back to the fence and the ladder and I am out of there. I hadn't realized how tense I was until I drive away. I am wet with perspiration and breathing rapidly. At home, it's five o'clock and there waiting for me in the living room is Gineen. She rushes at me and throws herself on me, nearly knocking me over.

"Hon, what in the world are you doing up?"

"Umm, I have been entertaining a few men. Please don't look in the closet or you'll embarrass them. Now quickly tell me how it went. Did you get into the mansion? Did you find anything? Are they chasing you?"

"Good, yes, yes, no."

"It's too early in the morning for that kind of silly humor."

"Alright. I did get into the Mansion and I did find something but at this point I don't know if it means anything. And no, I don't think anyone saw me and no one is following me."

"C'mon, I'll make you some breakfast," she offers as she puts her arm around my shoulder and starts to lead me toward the kitchen. "Hey, you're all wet. Is it raining out there?"

"No. I guess I was sweating a little bit."

"A little bit? Nonsense go take off that damp shirt while I get you some hot coffee and eggs. Where in the world did you get that jacket?"

"From a closet in the Mansion. I thought it might be useful for fiber analysis. Let's be careful not to contaminate it with fibers from here. A fresh plastic bag would be good."

"I'll get one while you take a hot shower. You may not know it, but you are shaking a little bit. Go."

The hot shower feels good. Gineen was right, I was shaking and not from the ambient air temperature. I shave while I'm at it and dress in some clean clothes. Back in the kitchen, I start to wolf down the eggs and bacon. The hot coffee warms my insides and I finally calm down.

"Thanks, sweetheart, you are so thoughtful."

"Stop that nonsense and show me what you found there.

What is it? Some paper records? Photographs? Maps? What?"

"Slow down. I'm not even sure that what I found is meaningful."

I take out the slip of paper with the telephone number and Amherst written on it. She looks and thinks a bit, her brow wrinkled. "Ah. Amherst, the site of the Laurence Swamp. Of course, it's connected and a powerful lead that will knock this case wide open."

"Maybe, but it might only be a girlfriend's number."

"You don't really believe that crap. Let's call and find out."

"Whoa. Slow down and let's think a little. If it's just a girlfriend or a boyfriend or a relative, there still might be a connection and we tip them off by calling it. Worse, they will be able to trace the call back to us. No way do we touch that phone. I'm thinking we should call in the state police and the feds before we make any kind of a move."

"There you go, spoiling all my fun. I had visions of driving out to Amherst and finding the bad guys and the lost artwork in one fell swoop."

"Sorry but we call Allen first and let him choose the next step which will likely be to call the group together and map out a plan."

"Committee work so far has resulted in nothing. Bah, I'm going upstairs to shower and dress."

I do the dishes and go into the office to think about possible next moves. It's very simple and straight forward. Any action from here depends on that phone number and who it belongs to. I am tempted to use a reverse telephone lookup but reject even that. I'll leave everything to the pros from here on in and I'll offer whatever assistance seems appropriate. Time to call Allen.

"Allen here."

"It's Patrick. We need to get together with our law enforcement crew."

"I suppose that means you got into the mansion last night and have found something."

"Good thinking, boss. Absolutely correct."

"And found something significant."

"I think, but I'm not sure and I think the cops should take the next steps."

"You are right. I'll get in touch with Wilson and crew and try to set up a meeting in my office this morning. You on board?"

"Yep, I'll be there with bells on. Call me when you can confirm a time."

An hour later he calls back and the meet is set for two at his office. This will give us a chance to hear all the evidence we have and put together a plan to wrap up this case. When I arrive, the group has assembled and indeed it has expanded to include another federal agency, the DEA. The head is Mark Adkind and we are all introduced. It's Allen's office, he convenes the meeting. He immediately takes control of the agenda.

"Gentlemen, we have some new evidence and analysis since our last meeting and I think it would be efficient to review where we are for Mr. Adkind. So, let's start with Patrick Ingel, my investigator on the art theft that started this ever-expanding mystery off in the first place. Patrick."

"I have obtained only one bit of information from the Brandt Mansion and that is a telephone number from Amherst, Mass, which is the town where Ponce's body was found. Ponce was the security guard at the Brandt Mansion at the time of the theft."

Adkind interrupts with, "And you obtained this number when and how?"

"Let me just say that Mr. Brandt doesn't know we have it." I can see from the look on his face that he has put two and two together and come up with the right answer, which doesn't please him at all. Too bad. There are a few stifled snickers from several other members of the group.

"I have done nothing with the number, not even called it to see who might answer. I figure how we treat it may affect how we proceed with the rest of the investigation. I am ready to help in any way I can with, of course, my client's approval."

I can see from the look on his face that Adkind would prefer that I go home right now. His attitude is in contrast with the other law enforcement guys at the table. As if to highlight this contrast, Wilson offers, "As usual, a good job, Patrick."

Allen continues, "For your information, Mr. Adkind, Patrick, has tracked the import of millions of dollars' worth of drugs to a man by the name of Karzai in San Francisco. He found out that the drugs are shipped to the port and then distributed, packaged in a Kia automobile and transported to a central location in Chicago by an auto shipping company named Brown and Company. There they are repackaged in street-sized volume. From there, we believe the drugs are sold nationwide. For sure, Agent Adkind, we have a roadmap of the travel of the drugs from the point they are shipped from Afghanistan to Chicago. Doesn't leave a lot for you to do but scoop up these guys and put them away for good. Of course," Allen adds, "we have nothing to do with the drugs in this case, and we are only concerned with the theft of the art."

"You make it sound so simple, but it is likely to be more complicated than that."

"Sure, Agent Adkind, and we certainly are at your service and will help any way we can."

Taking the focus off the jerk, Wilson volunteers the following, "I am putting one of our detectives on the Amherst telephone number right now. It shouldn't take us long to find who the listing belongs to and an address to go along with it. We'll then look at the owner and check into his or her background as far as we can go."

"Excellent," says Allen.

"And the FBI will see what they can learn about the identity of the new security guard at the mansion with our facial recognition software," Wilson says. "In addition, I want our lab to learn what they can from the coat you snitched from the Mansion. Any idea which one of the residents it belongs to?"

"Yeah. It's a pricey jacket and I'm guessing it fits Brandt just fine. On the other hand, I still doubt that he would do any of the dirty work himself."

"With all this work staring us in the face, it looks like we should adjourn and reconvene when we have more to go on. Our focus seems to be zeroing in on the Amherst telephone. Thanks for taking the risk for obtaining that data, Patrick." This from Wilson and I suspect he is rubbing it in purposefully to irritate Adkind. Good for him. Everyone starts to leave but Allen holds me back until they all leave his office.

"Any more ideas, Patrick?"

"Not really, just raring to go and I'd like nothing better than to rush out to the place in Amherst. Good I don't know where it is, or I'd be getting in the way of the state police."

"Somehow I have a feeling that they might like to have you along when they first go to size up the place. We'll see. Give Gineen a squeeze for me."

"I will. Later."

I stop on the way home and get two pizzas for lunch. One for me with everything on it and one for Gineen with organic veggies and tofu on it. She has waited for me to start lunch, so we set the table and dig into the pizza.

"Oh yum, I am so starved that I could eat both these pizzas if one of them didn't have all that disgusting stuff on it. Alright out with it. How did the meeting go?"

"Before I get into that I need a beer. Is there any in the fridge"?

"Of course, there's at least one six pack of a local craft brew. I'll get one for you."

"No, no, you sit still, and I'll get it." I retrieve a beer, pop the cap off, and return to Gineen. "OK, let me go over the latest happenings. Tim took over control of the meeting from the start and everything went smoothly except for one asshole from the DEA who just came in from Washington and couldn't spit in the ocean if he were bobbing around on it in an inner tube. All the rest of the troop was grateful to have the Amherst telephone number and we are focusing on that. Once the state police check it out, we will reconvene but that likely won't be until tomorrow morning."

"Good that means the investigation is all but closed, and you are mine again. Yummy."

"Yummy? Not really. Tim thinks the FBI and state police

will want me to go with them when they get more info on the Amherst telephone number. So, I'm not quite out of it yet. Don't forget recovering the art works is still my area."

"Bummer. A newly minted father should not be going out in the field and taking risks."

"Gineen, you don't know if you are pregnant and we've had this conversation before. I'm a detective. It's what I do. It's what I've done since you met me."

"I know but you can't blame me for trying to protect my man, can you?"

"No, I don't. But on the other hand, don't overdo it. Now finish your pizza and let's go upstairs and make sure you are pregnant, for certain."

It's fair to say that a good time is had by all. Even without caviar and champagne. My breakfast is interrupted by a call from Allen.

"Sorry to call so early but the team is raring to go. We are going to assemble in my office this morning in one hour. Can you make it?"

"A little tight but I'll be there."

I arrive just as the group is sitting down to coffee and donuts provided by Tim. No jokes about police and donuts do I hear, and I wisely decline to make any.

Tim has given up the leadership role now that what we all hope will be the final action in this maze of mysteries. Wilson of the state police takes over.

"Alright everyone we do have some new information that we need to share with you. First our lab guys confirm that some fibers and soil samples on the jacket Patrick provided match those found at the scene. Of course, we don't know for sure whose jacket it is but by the size it is a good fit for

Swazey. We called the mansion last night with fairytale stories asking for him, and were told he was not in. We had an observer watching the mansion last night and no one left the place after he arrived. Just to make sure that he was not in the mansion, we called again this morning with the same tale. Told again that he was not at home. Without searching the place, we don't know for sure that he is gone but that is our working assumption until we find out otherwise. The indications are that he is our murderer. The facial recognition programs did ID the new security guard. He has a shady past and has served a short term in a local jail in New York State for a breaking and entering some years ago but has been clean since them. He's a tough guy who exercises and lifts weights every single day. He has some tats from his jail days. We don't consider him to be a suspect for any crime but if he's near, be careful. He shouldn't have a licensed firearm due to his record but that doesn't mean his hasn't obtained one.

"Swazey is our principal suspect, so we ran his name through the local tax assessor's records to see if he had any property registered in his name. No luck, but when we searched for any family in the area, we found that his mother had several listings there. We established which of the two she lived in and that left us with the one where we think Swazey is hiding out. It's a small log cabin affair deep in the woods adjacent to the Laurence Swamp. The cabin is sited at the end of a long dirt access road making it impossible to see the cabin from the point where the drive leaves the access road which is also unpaved. This is a very isolated area with no neighbors for miles around. We have stationed a lookout at the end of the drive to make sure he doesn't leave if, in fact, he is there. We have a full swat team holed up at the Amherst P.D., ready to go into action when we give them the word. That, gentlemen, is where we stand now, as far as the state is concerned, except we do have a search warrant for the Brandt mansion since that is his official residence. We will go in there and the log cabin simultaneously."

"And we will be raiding your garage in Chicago at the same time," says Adkind with a big smirk on his face as if all this was his doing.

I check in at this point in the discussion. "Gentlemen, at this point my major interest is in the stolen art works so I would like to be at the cabin when you go in. If it's there I will be able to identify it and look after it. And remember at this point my client and I are the only ones who have seen Swazey in person."

"The DEA cannot go along with that," pipes up Adkind in a commanding voice.

"Not your call," overrules Wilson forcefully. "This is our operation."

Adkind is livid but holds his temper in check. Wilson looks at me with a stern look on his face. "Patrick you can go along with the proviso that you stay in the background until we have secured the site. Got it?"

"You're the boss."

"We are going to set this up to begin at four a.m. tomorrow morning so y'all go home and get some sleep. We meet at the Amherst P.D. and go from there," Wilson says.

At the condo Gineen greets me with a big hug, eager to know what transpired at the meeting.

"I think you should be on Tim's payroll. You probably would have more good ideas than some on our team, notably, the DEA jerk. We are set to attack tomorrow morning at four a.m. in Amherst, so I'll be out of here at two. That doesn't leave me much time to sleep so let's eat dinner and I'll be off to sleep right away."

"No time for love?"

"Are you kidding. I need my strength. All this running back and forth to Amherst is wearing me out. We get a long vacation when this is all over. Remember that!"

"I'll hold you to that, I promise. Imagine that. Weeks without any mysteries staring us in the face. I vote for a nice warm beach somewhere."

"We decide that when it's time. I'm off to bed."

At one thirty I am showered, dressed and in the car when Gineen shouts at me from the open door. "Hey, I made you a breakfast sandwich to eat on the way." I get out of the car and meet her halfway to the door. I hug her and thank her and I'm off. I purposely didn't want her to come to the car where she might have seen my pistol that I had stowed on the floor in front of the passenger seat. I don't carry a gun very often, but something told me to take it along today. Traffic is very light this time of the morning and I make good time on the Mass Pike and arrive in plenty of time for lift off. I am wearing a loose windbreaker with my gun inside my belt at my back.

"OK, guys this is it," says Wilson. It is 3:45 a.m. "Patrick, you stay well back in your car and remember, don't go anywhere near that cabin until we have secured it and given you the signal."

We arrive at the end of the driveway at about 3:55 and Wilson, true to his word, waits until exactly 4:00 when he waves his troop forward slowly and quietly. When they get within sight of the cabin, he signals the guys to go down on the ground and keep still.

"What can you see, Pete?" he says to the guy next to him.

"No sign of anybody and all of the lights are out. There's a pickup truck parked next to the cabin. Looks like a small Chevy. Can't see the plate but it fits the description of Swazey's truck, I think."

"Check it out with headquarters to make sure." They wait another five minutes until the truck is confirmed to be Swazey's. By that time the sky is lightening, and visibility is rapidly increasing. Wilson waves a couple of guys around to the rear of the cabin and another two to the sides, effectively surrounding the place.

While this is going on, I am waiting patiently out by the end of the drive. I have studied the aerial photos of the site and have seen what looks like a trail leading off from the back of the cabin into the woods. I decide to check that out and walk carefully up to the point where it crosses the road.

At that moment, I hear a voice on a bullhorn ordering the cabin occupants to open the door. When there is no response a loud cracking noise breaks the silence. I take that to be a ramrod taking down door, and that is followed by a cacophony of voices shouting orders and commands. No response from the cabin. At that moment, I see a shadowy figure cross the dirt road ahead of me and slither off to the right.

I chase him down the path, and when I start to get close, I realize he is pushing an off-road vehicle down the slight grade. He is about to jump on and start the bloody thing up, so I shout at him to stop in the name of the law. Well, a slight exaggeration. He turns toward me, and I see him raise his arm which is followed by loud crack of a gun as a bullet whizzes close by my head. That's it. I assume a three-point stance and get off two shots to the fat tires on the back of the thing. Both shots hit their targets, the tires go flat, the vehicle slews around and tips over. I run over to the overturned vehicle and turn the driver over onto his stomach with a knee in his back. He's breathing but stunned enough so that he doesn't offer any resistance. I slip a pair of plastic cuffs over his wrists.

It's Swazey. Wilson and crew come running up and he lifts me off Swazey and gives me a playful tap on my shoulder. "Nice going, Patrick."

"It's nothing," I say as though I do it every day. "What did you find in the cabin?"

"Let's go back. We hadn't gotten into the place before we heard the shots and came running over."

Two members of the state police haul Swazey to his feet and drag him back to the cabin. The door has been devastated by the battering ram, so we walk inside after Swazey has been locked up in the back seat of a cruiser. Inside the cabin, we find nothing of value – some clothes, food in the fridge. No computer but there is an iPhone which Wilson puts in an evidence bag. The lab crew arrives and begins its job of collecting samples of fibers, hair, and DNA.

"They will be here for several hours. Let's go talk to Swazey. Maybe he will have something helpful to say before he gets all lawyered up."

Wilson reads him his rights. His only response is no response at all.

"I got nothing to say to you guys. Out here on vacation and you bust in and scare the living daylights out of me. You got nothing on me. I want a lawyer."

We drive back to the Amherst Police Station where they throw Swazey into a cell. He makes his one call and then sneers at Wilson, "You got nothing on me."

"Surprise, we have enough on you to send you to prison for life. To say nothing of this iPhone that we found inside."

At the mention of the cell his sneer turns to a look of fear. There must be something incriminating on it.

"I guess you don't mind if our lab guys see what's on it." Wilson sees what I see. "You sure you wouldn't like to make a statement now?"

The wheels turn in Swazey's head and I think I can almost hear them. There is a prolonged silence and then he slumps back in the seat. "Listen, I have what you want but you must make a deal with me."

"I don't make deals with killers, Swazey. The best I can offer you is a promise that if you cooperate with the state, I will pass that along to the prosecutor, maybe resulting in a lighter sentence. But that's not up to me."

Swazey is put into an interrogation room and left alone for a half an hour.

"We'll let him sweat for a while, so he knows we are serious. Come on, we'll treat you to some police station coffee and a few stale donuts."

Wilson keeps him sweating another thirty minutes while we occasionally peek at him through the one-way glass. He stares at the one-way glass. Clearly knows we are watching, and this seems to increase the tension. Finally, Wilson decides that it's enough and says, "OK, let's go talk. He appears to be ripe."

In the interrogation room, he begins with another threat, "Before we get started, Swazey, just remember, most of what you are going to tell us we already know, so play it straight with us. We have an iron-clad murder case against you and since it is also a federal case. The death penalty can be enforced. Look up at the camera and tell us in your own words everything you know about the scheme to murder Ponce, including the motive. Talk."

"It's easy. I was ordered to get rid of Ponce by Brandt. He threatened to have his new security guard wipe me off the face of the earth unless I did it. My reward was to be a bonus of $25,000 in cash if I did the job and didn't get caught. I was planning to use the cash to pay the way for me to get out of Brandt's clutches and disappear. I realize now, that he probably never intended to pay me at all but to have the new guard take me out and hide my remains."

"Do you have anything in writing to confirm this?"

"No. All I have are the phone records of my calls to him which you already have."

"Are you absolutely sure that you have nothing at all in writing from Brandt. A note, a check, an email?"

"Nah. He's too smart for a dumb move like that."

"And why did he want Ponce dead?"

"He didn't tell me directly, but the word was that Ponce was trying to get Brandt to pay him five million dollars or give him the supposedly stolen art works which Brandt has stashed away."

I interrupt as this point, "Do you have any idea where the art is hidden?"

"Not exactly but I have a notion that I'd be willing to share with you in return for your help in disappearing from here so his friends can't get at me."

"Nonsense. There is no way in the world we can let you go

scot free with a murder conviction just about guaranteed."

I want whatever he has that might locate the art, so I ask, "Is there a way you can give him a false ID, remove the death penalty, and hold him in some remote facility?"

"We might be able to get the DA to agree to this. We would make the recommendation to him and under the circumstances, I rather think he will buy it."

"What do you say, Swazey?" I ask.

"We have a deal. Like I say, I don't know for sure, but the word is that Brandt has a lavish summer place on Lake Winnipesaukee in New Hampshire, and that is where I would look first. I heard that it is guarded year-round, so the art would be secure there. I just don't know exactly where it is."

I think this is good stuff, so I add this, "I can get Tim Allen to search the tax records for Carrol and Belknap Counties, and it should be easy for him to find the place."

"Do you think he would check this out right now?"

"Are you kidding? To get rid of a five-million-dollar claim, he'd check it out on Christmas Eve. It would be a great Christmas present for him if it pans out. Let me call him right now."

I do and of course, he is thrilled to go to work after I explain the situation. He promises to call back within an hour. I can just picture him calling in some overdue favors. Feeling more than generous, I offer to go out and bring back some breakfast for all of us. Wilson directs me to a breakfast joint not far away. I drive over to it and load up scrambled eggs, bacon, coffee, and some fresh donuts and bring it back to the station. In the middle of wolfing my portion down, I am interrupted by my cell. It is Allen.

"OK, the place is in Wolfeboro on the east side of the lake. It's a lavish lakeside home with its own dock, tennis courts, and two acres of lawn that slope down to the water. More than enough area to land a helicopter. Can Wilson get in touch with the New Hampshire State Police and arrange a group to drop in on this hideaway which incidentally is owned by one of Brandt's companies? And I want you to be part of that group. I can have a copter pick you up in a couple of hours and fly you to the home."

Phew, he is really working overtime. "We will be waiting."

I respond to Wilson's quizzical look with, "I hope I didn't commit you to something that you can't do but I told Allen that we could fly up to Wolfeboro, New Hampshire and meet some New Hampshire State Policemen for a raid in a couple of hours."

"Ha. I wouldn't miss it for the world. Let me arrange for a raid on Brandt's mansion for the same time that we will be at the lake." He makes the arrangements and less than two hours later Allen's copter arrives and we make the flight up to Wolfeboro. As we descend to a spot next to the house, I am impressed by the aerial view of this lavish summer "cottage."

Wilson, with the help of two New Hampshire State Policemen, quickly subdue the single security guard and we enter the place and begin searching for the art. It doesn't take long to find it in a small upstairs room with nothing else in it. Wilson takes possession of it and signs a receipt for it. Allen has arranged for the copter to fly me back to Boston and then take Wilson back to Amherst. We shake hands after we land at Logan and he pats me on the back and says, "Good job. If you every want to join law enforcement, give me a call."

"Good working with you. I think a long vacation is in order and I think I am going to become a dad, sometime in the next eight or nine months, so I can't take you up on that offer. You take care."

I rent a car at Logan and drive home to the condo. I open the door and shout at the top of my lungs, "IT'S OVER!"

Gineen is in the office and flies into my arms. "Oh, God, I am so happy to hear that news. Now on to the next project."

"I got news for you. The next project is a long vacation and work on becoming a dad."

"Oh super. I can help with both of those."

Later in the day, I call Allen and thank him for the job. I tell him about the long vacation we are planning, and he thinks it is a well-earned one. He suggests that I get back to him when I am ready to start work again.

THE END

www.ingramcontent.com/pod-product-compliance
Lightning Source LLC
Chambersburg PA
CBHW020446270626
47155CB00022B/1708